DAWN OF THE LIVING PROOF
Neighborlee Book 11

Michelle L. Levigne

www.YeOldeDragonBooks.com

Ye Olde Dragon Books
P.O. Box 30802
Middleburg Hts., OH 44130

www.YeOldeDragonBooks.com

2OldeDragons@gmail.com

Welcome to Neighborlee, Ohio.

Where? Somewhere on the North Coast of Ohio, south of Cleveland, right off I-71, north of Medina, in the heart of Cuyahoga County.

What is it? That's a little harder to explain.

Neighborlee is a place you need to experience.

The most important thing you need to understand: Neighborlee is *magic*. Some people say the town is alive. It exists to protect the weird and wonderful (and sometimes a little bit scary) from the cold, practical, material world.

More important, Neighborlee protects the outside world from the weird and wonderful that come to visit … and sometimes come to stay.

First stop: Divine's Emporium, a four-story Victorian house sitting on a hill overlooking the Metroparks. Whatever you really need, you can find at Divine's. Even if you don't know what you're looking for when you walk in the door. The shop is often bigger inside than it is outside. Angela is the proprietor. Please stay on the first floor. You don't want to find out what is hidden and locked safely away upstairs. Like Aslan, Angela is good, but that doesn't mean she's safe. And neither are the secrets and wonders and doorways to other worlds that she protects … and keeps securely locked.

Come in and explore. Meet the people who help Angela guard Neighborlee. Share their adventures of magic and wonder, danger and sacrifice. You never know who or what you'll run into as you walk the streets and listen to the stories of their lives.

Chapter One

"Who invited the Men in Black convention?" my brother Harry said, passing me on his way to the buffet. For the third time already this evening, and it was barely past 9pm. on New Year's Eve.

Harry Zephyr, Hispanic good looks, to differentiate him from white-blonde, geeky-hunky Harry who was in love with Bethany Miller, and also attending the New Year's Eve party at Eden, our community center. Specifically, Bethany's Harry was magic. As in pure-blood Fae. And yeah, I could see his pointed ears through that blonde hair. I'm pointing this out at the beginning so people don't get confused as the story progresses.

"Huh?" I nearly got out of my wheelchair, to turn around and see where he gestured with a lift of his elbow and a sideways tip of his curly dark head. He had his hands full, after all.

My legs had been prickly-tingly-jittery for days. It was escalating enough that I honestly couldn't blame the regenerating nerves and the growing reservoir of defensive energy filling Neighborlee, after dealing with some interdimensional nasties trying to drain the magic and punch a hole through to other realms.

I got myself turned around and looked at the small cluster of men, and possibly some women, judging by the slimmer shapes, standing by the doors into the big gym. Thanks to odd events over the last few years, the organizers of this year's party had wisely chosen not to have an overnighter or a lock-in. But still, why were outsiders crashing the party? Technically, they weren't crashing because they wouldn't have been allowed to get two steps inside the foyer without paying the entry fee. We had more than enough food for last-minute registrations. Still, these guys stood out like a black-and-blue thumb, in their black suits, black fedoras, black hard-sole shoes, and black sunglasses. Seriously? Sunglasses indoors? Granted, Stingray could get away with wearing sunglasses indoors, but he was (sigh) Stingray. There was a matter of style involved.

These guys weren't stylish by any means.

"Nope," I said after a couple seconds. "Men in Black have some style. These guys look like they raided the Salvation Army store and didn't try anything on before they left."

I was smart enough not to turn so I wasn't looking directly at the strangers in their ill-fitting clothes. Too big, so their cuffs went to their fingertips and their hats sat low over their ears. Like they were trying to hide something.

"Blues Brothers convention?" Harry had turned his back to them, too, so if they were looking our way, they couldn't tell we were talking about them.

"Akroyd would be rolling over in his grave if he saw them."

"Akroyd isn't dead." Harry sighed and grinned, catching on a few seconds too late that I was giving him a hard time.

Hey, I had to warm up in preparation for my required community service time, aka half an hour of comedy.

"Think there's a chance someone on the committee hired -- " He turned to look over his shoulder, frowned, and turned around all the way. "Weird."

"Be more specific." I turned my wheelchair around and understood what had my brother speechless.

The out-of-style Men in Black had completely vanished.

My fingers tingled, another side-effect and questionable benefit of the build-up of defensive energy. Two seconds after that, one of the Hounds that protected Stanzer and Dawn materialized out of thin air. Granted, their usual way of entering a room. Scattering blue sparks of energy, the oversized big bad black wolfish beastie walked through two tables and proceeded to sniff along the wall by the doors, where the strangers had been maybe thirty seconds ago. I had no proof, but gut instinct said they had vanished because they had done something to attract the attention of the Hound. Were they here because of Stanzer and Dawn?

Stanzer, our local PI, had been searching for years to find his own version of Lost Kids, called the Hunt. They were sent from their home in another dimension, to protect them from a galactic despot. They had been scattered through time, so they didn't arrive on Earth all at once or all together. Dawn was the first one Stanzer had found. They were set up in the building he had bought to use as a headquarters and guarded by the Hounds. These interdimensional guardian beasts kind of scared me, even though they'd saved my bacon a few times. Perhaps adding the Hounds to the defenses of Neighborlee had made me a little too ready to goof off and enjoy myself on New Year's Eve.

Despite the history of Eden and New Year's Eve in Neighborlee.

An invasion at three hours until the magic hour was not how I wanted to bring in the new year, thanks very much.

Of course, Harry didn't see the Hound. He was watching me with that frown that meant he expected me to explain things. How, when I had no answers yet? Mum and Pop had managed to hold onto the magical energy they had absorbed after getting yanked forward almost two years from the Bermuda Triangle, back home to Neighborlee. Harry and Pete were our family's token ordinary mortals, and while they had been able to see and hear Maurice, our visiting exiled Fae, that had been temporary. Both had experienced enough weirdness over the years, they could tell when the guardians were bracing to face the newest threat to our weird little town. I had hopes that eventually, both my brothers would absorb enough magic to eventually see and hear things so I wouldn't have to keep explaining or translating.

After all, Holly could now see and hear Maurice. She was another Lost Kid without superpowers, but she had enough magic in her blood, she and Maurice might just have a chance at a happily-ever-after. Once his term of punishment had ended and he was released from being shrunk down to five inches tall, with shrunken magic and wings slapped on his back even Tinkerbell wouldn't be caught dead in.

"Where are Dawn and Stanzer?" I asked, watching the Hound.

Harry pointed at a round table two tables away from the one we shared with our folks, the Longfellows, and Pastor Rocky. I had been sitting with my back to it, so I hadn't seen them. Sighing, I turned my chair around and had to resist the urge to give a really hard mental shove. My wheelchair was why we took the table on the outer edge of the room. Traffic was awful, with people going to the buffet tables or raffle prize tables on the far end of the room, to put their tickets in the bags. Plus the people selling the tickets were wandering everywhere, in and out between tables. We were taking a break between scheduled activities, so everybody could just sit and talk and eat. Gina and her staff had outdone themselves, as usual, with the spread of food.

I slalomed my way between the tables, stopping every other chair to return greetings with friends and neighbors and co-workers. What should have taken me maybe five minutes took fifteen, giving me time to reflect on all we had lived through, all the reasons we had for celebrating.

New Year's Eve at Eden. That should have been the first warning to bring in the new year quietly and privately. I, at least, should have had some premonition or just a bit of paranoia. Despite the healing in my spine, obviously my ability to see in the future hadn't grown or improved. After all, we had had more than our fair share of weird events at Eden, and not just at New Year's.

However, that year I was just feeling too dang good, and so was everyone I knew. We were justified in cutting loose and relaxing and being silly. Hadn't we earned it?

Retrieving Mum and Pop from the Bermuda Triangle had let us give a major rap on the knuckles to some nasties. Starting with a vampish chick named Kerri, who had tried to trick me and Pete into signing a nasty magical contract that would have given her a foothold in Neighborlee. It turned out she had been threatening Mum and Pop during their stay in Bermuda two years ago. Everything tied into some presumably charmed beads found by Pete's birth-mother, Emma. Hopefully, after the double whammy we gave Kerri and her goons last summer, they were still curled up under a really heavy rock somewhere, licking their wounds.

We knew better than to believe she was gone for good. She was just regaining her strength and plotting new strategies, just like Big Ugly, who had been threatening Neighborlee for decades. When our enemies struck again, we would be more prepared than ever. We had two powerful allies now. First, Hoax, Inc., the organization that had raised Jane. Then there was the network of other Lost Kids and their descendants, headed by Arthur Sheridan, Daniel's grandfather, scion of the Sheridan Communications organization.

On a whole lot of positive notes: Athena and Wallace had finally set a date and were planning their wedding. Major accomplishment in their relationship. Pessimists were sure they were going to quietly take a step back and dis-engage, that Wallace had proposed just to protect Athena from the misguided ideas of romance being flung at her by Freddie Grandstone.

But no, Wallace was serious. He had proved it with a really cool ring Angela helped him pick out. And proved it more by getting approval from Ford and Charlotte. I was happy for them.

Bethany was home and considering fleeing the ego-driven rat race of Hollywood -- and she had found her faerie prince charming, Harry. He was a really great guy, and a lot of fun to hang with. The two of them were good for each other, and I was delighted to have both of my girls spoken for and paired up with guys who would take care of them.

Felicity and Jake were still coasting along in newlywed bliss after more than a year. Gordon and Mandy Priebe had just had their one-year anniversary. The overbearing in-law problems had pretty much melted away. The threat of a Star Trek-themed wedding had tamed all those loving-but-obtuse folks who might otherwise have tried to run their lives for them. Starting with pressuring Mandy and Gordon to start popping out babies. Excuse me? They were both in their upper thirties, and while modern medicine could protect against the medical problems that came with later-in-life babies, they also had the Lost Kids heritage to worry about.

Athena and Doni Longfellow and Bethany Miller were wonderful examples of the good that could come from a Lost Kids heritage. However, we were still sorting through the wreckage of the Rivals' organization and learning more about the pretty horrific things they had done to Lost Kids, to control their semi-pseudo-superhero abilities. Um, no thanks. If I ever got married, I would be hesitant about bringing a new generation of Lost Kids into the world. I love little kids, proven by the fact I was still teaching Sunday school, but I preferred to keep them in the fill-them-with-sugar-and-send-them-home category.

Where was I when this diatribe started? Oh, yeah, counting our blessings.

Jon-Tom and Jeri Castle and Diane and Troy Richards were home from their honeymoons. Our newlyweds were safely within the borders of Neighborlee, sheltered from any residual weirdness that might try to sabotage their happily-ever-afters.

My younger brother Pete and Meggie Richards were looking more serious every day, despite the stresses and strains of being full-time students at Willis-Brooks College.

Most important of all, I was pretty sure from the edgy-nervous looks Kurt kept giving Jane, and the way he kept checking his pocket where he didn't keep his cell phone, he had finally gotten up the nerve to use that engagement ring I knew he had bought shortly after Jane settled in Neighborlee.

The biggest item on my gratitude list? My legs were getting more feeling back in them. In the privacy of my house, and the gym Jake had built in the basement of his and Felicity's house, I was doing exercises to strengthen them. Too often, the regenerating nerves just made my legs jittery. I still couldn't trust them to hold me up for more than walking around my kitchen or housecleaning. I certainly wasn't going to freak out the people of our town by going to work and going shopping without my wheelchair. Not yet. Not until I had a doctor's certificate proclaiming a medical miracle.

Bottom line: I was going to take the final phase of my long-delayed healing very slowly, very carefully. And when I could leave my wheelchair up on blocks in the back yard, I was going to have an entire wardrobe of spiffy canes to play with, until I was entirely steady and walking on my own, with no threatened relapses of numbness and shaking and unreliable joints.

This New Year's Eve, the festivities had been toned down. Not just because of the economy and world events. The guardians had been enforcing the message to the people in authority: No more caging the people of Neighborlee in one location for too long. The doors were open, but watched by a few security officers to make sure nobody and nothing nasty came in.

Other than those weirdoes who were either Blues Brothers groupies or wannabe Men in Black. Where had they gone? And why was that Hound still nosing around along the wall where they had been standing? Should I be worried that it wasn't following their trail? Should I be relieved it hadn't moved on? And how come none of the other guardians had seen it? They weren't that busy eating and playing those puzzle games, intent on winning some really spiffy door prizes, were they?

It was New Year's Eve, and the guardians of Neighborlee were on duty, as always. We knew how to relax and still have fun and give the general impression that we weren't worried. Too much, anyway. Maybe everyone expected everyone else to be paying attention, and I was the only one with my head up and my eyes open, to notice?

I was relieved, more than I had been just twenty minutes ago, that the party was only scheduled to go until 1am. Then everyone could go home and dive into bed and sleep like sane people. Felicity and Jake were having people over for an after-party. I had tentative plans to go, but only if Daniel didn't go. Honestly? He was giving me some weird, considering looks. Like he couldn't decide if he was about to die, or pull a messy, hilariously embarrassing trick on me. The guy was making me edgy enough to get up out of my chair and try dancing.

Mum and Pop weren't planning to stay up until dawn, and I was very happy to follow their example. Yeah, I was starting to feel a little old. Well, save the world from invasion from the dungeon dimensions a couple times every year, it starts adding up and weighing down even a semi-pseudo-superhero.

Besides, Pete had moved back in with Mum and Pop, so I had the house entirely to myself once again. Bliss!

Finally, I got to Stanzer and Dawn's table, and could pull my head out of my circling thoughts. Before they turned into a downward spiral. Weird, I know, but when I got through the crowd of people blocking my view, and I saw neither of them were at their table, I was relieved. It meant they were on the alert.

Unless the Men in Black/Blues Brothers fans had gotten hold of them? But wouldn't the Hound be on the attack? Unless these guys were so powerful that --

"Hey, what's up?" Dawn stepped around me and put two cups of punch down at the two open spots at the table. Stanzer was right behind her, carrying two plates.

His smile faded the longer he looked at me. I had hooked my thumb over my shoulder, toward the doorway. He looked, stood up straight, and all the tight lines in his face that had faded away in the months since Dawn came to Neighborlee were back. He was on the alert.

Dawn muttered something that sounded foreign and took the plates from Stanzer's hands, put them on the table, and gestured at the doorway with a lift of her chin. She opened her mouth, then frowned and didn't say what I thought would be a question. Somewhere along the lines of: Do we go after them?

I turned to look. The Hound was gone.

"What did you see?" Stanzer stepped around me to pull out one of the chairs. He leaned on it while Dawn settled into it, and we had a huddle right there, in the middle of all the happy New Year's Eve chatter and laughter.

I told them. Neither of them looked quite as grim as I expected. I wanted so much for that to be a good sign. Gee, it was a good thing I didn't drink anything stronger than kombucha or an occasional hard cider. My brain circuits were fried enough as it was.

"We have to assume the danger is past, if the Hound left," Stanzer said.

"Or it's chasing them," Dawn said. He nodded.

"Or whoever they are, they're not looking for you two, specifically, anymore," I said.

"That's ... a good idea," Stanzer said, nodding slowly. The guy was starting to look like a bobblehead. "The Hounds like you and the other guardians, but they're not focused on protecting you. Unless there's a threat to you that includes us." He straightened up and looked around the gym, and weariness seemed to settle on him like a heavy hooded cloak. "I think I need to have a look around. Maybe talk with some of our friends."

Two choices. Either he would try to get a Hound to come back and communicate with him what was up, or he would walk the perimeter of Eden and check with the security detail. Since the Sheridan Corporation was sponsoring tonight's party, that meant Sheridan employees and allies, most of them with special gifts from their Lost Kids ancestry. That was comforting, but not as much as I would have liked. If the guards hadn't detected trouble when the Blues Brother cosplayers came into the building, then these people might be more dangerous than they looked. Physical and maybe metaphysical danger, rather than just a threat to our sanity. I really hoped Stanzer checked with security, because trying to talk to the Hounds, especially when they didn't want to "talk," could be exhausting.

He paused long enough to give Dawn a look that clearly said for her to stay put, and then he walked away. She scowled and hunched her shoulders, then made a visible effort to cheer up.

"Are you two okay?" I asked. Which was really a stupid question, because they were betrothed, back when he was only four years older than her. Here on Earth, he was twelve years older than Dawn, and the pressure was heavy to be patient and not do something stupid. She was a high school student and he was her legal guardian.

"It really isn't that romantic to have a white knight looking after you," she muttered. "And things are just going to get worse when more of the Hunt show up and they're still kids."

I stopped myself in time from trying to cheer her up by theorizing that maybe they would be married and have kids by the time someone else showed up. Nope, that would not be encouraging. When I suggested she come back to my table with me, she agreed. She was probably thinking the same thing I was, that Stanzer would want me to look after her. It had to be rough for Dawn, the new kid in town, knowing she was capable of defending herself, and everyone treating her like she was just a kid. She had certainly proven herself clever and a good fighter when she had helped take down a major crime boss last summer.

Dawn settled into the seat that Daniel had asked me to save for him two hours ago. He was busy running a lot of things behind the scenes. Like security and helping Gina and her team of miracle workers. It was nice that she could sit back and enjoy the evening for longer than two or three minutes at a time, and it kept Daniel away and busy.

I focused on having fun right here and now at the party. Because I was determined it was going to be the best in years.

My comedy routine went off perfectly. No interruptions. No weirdness. No reappearance of the Men in Black/Blues Brothers wannabes. Stanzer returned and he and Dawn settled at our table. We had plenty of room.

We had the raffle drawing, divided up into ten-minute segments on the hour, to allow people to go into side rooms to play games. We had our traditional game of Murder in the small gym. Hey, the stupid game was a tradition for New Year's Eve. Besides, this year, I had canes hidden in a few places, so I could ditch my wheelchair and get around on my own feet for short distances, and really freak out people. If I drew the "m" ticket to make me the Murderer. Which didn't happen this year.

Then at 11:30, all other activities shut down and everyone reconvened in the big gym, to draw a few more raffle prizes and wait for the ball drop. Kurt had promised this year's light display for the countdown would be even more spectacular than ever.

When things turned weird, Pop was up on the stage with Pastor Rocky and Ford Longfellow and the rest of their retro rock-n-roll band. Mum was walking the edges of the crowd, getting pictures and chatting with people. She had truly lived up to her name, managing to dye her hair in multicolored stripes that seemed to move on their own as she walked through one colored spotlight stream after another. That was fine, that was fun, and pretty normal. Until ...

"He's going for it," Felicity squeaked, reaching across Daniel to grab my arm.

I had no idea when he got there. I had been focusing on the band and indulging in a little more reminiscing.

"Who's going for what?" I asked.

Felicity pointed and I followed the line of her finger, to the door out into the lobby. For a second there, I thought the Blues Brothers were back, and Stanzer was facing them down. Hopefully not with a Hound on either side of him, which would mean these cosplayers or whatever they were had come to make trouble.

Nope. Not them. Just Kurt and Jane, out beyond the doors, in the lobby.

I squeaked. I couldn't help it. Kurt was down on one knee in front of Jane and she was starting to go invisible. Yeah, that was shock. Maybe turning invisible was a survival technique.

Maybe she felt Felicity and me and everyone else at our table turning to look at them. Kurt turned, very obviously feeling our attention and how we were silently cheering him on. He scowled for about two seconds, then it turned into a grin as he caught hold of Jane's hand and they both turned invisible.

"Darn, I didn't even get to see the ring. He did have a ring in his pocket, didn't he?" Felicity grumbled.

"He did," Angela said. Her voice was almost a purr. "More important, he went to Hoax and had a long talk with Demetrius and Beau and the other elders, getting their blessing."

"Good for him." Jake chuckled and raised his glass of cranberry punch. "I was kind of relieved I didn't have to go through that when we got engaged --"

"Who says you didn't?" I retorted and fluttered my eyelashes at him. "Do you think Kurt and I would have let you hang around Felicity as long as you did if we didn't approve of you for our little sister?"

"And you passed the test with us," Mum said, showing up at just the right time to hear the end of the conversation. She settled into an empty seat beside Angela, rested her chin on her clasped hands, elbows on the table, and showed where I had learned to flutter my eyelashes in a teasing-yet-threatening fashion.

Jake groaned, then laughed a little. "I stand corrected."

"Hey." Kurt and Jane popped into view between our table and the wall. "Something's going on." He rubbed his fingers together, our signal since childhood that he felt some otherworldly or semi-pseudo-superhero power at work.

Then he pointed at Daniel.

"Who's that?"

"Hey, been hitting the sauce a little early?" Daniel said.

That wasn't Daniel's voice. Something raspy about it.

Besides, he wouldn't joke about Kurt drinking. And for another thing, this was a family-friendly event, kids of all ages were encouraged to attend, so no alcohol allowed in the entire building. Other than the first aid kits. And the cherries jubilee.

"Go. A. Way," Felicity growled, as green and pink sparks filled her eyes and rolled off the ends of her curls.

Daniel stumbled to his feet, shoving the chair back so it collapsed with a bang that was pretty much muffled by all the talking and laughing and music around us. Nobody turned to look. Good thing, because Felicity leaped from her chair and grabbed hold of the imposter's arm as he kind of melted around the edges. A look of utter horror twisted his face into something like Munsch's *Scream* as he looked past the far end of the table. Despite knowing better, I turned to look.

To see Daniel, the real Daniel, come running, staggering every third step. Poisonous yellow sparks swarmed around his head, like really nasty, winter-defying bees.

"Let go of him," Felicity growled, and turned on the juice, adding purple sparks to the ones already there. They swirled down her arm to her hand holding the duplicate's arm.

The fake Daniel let out this scream that I swear sounded like the Wicked Witch of the West as she melted from the bucket of water Dorothy threw on her, only speeded up. Then he vanished with a visible but silent pop. Fortunately, no smoke, no other sound effects. Just like always, the Neighborlee defensive magic came through and nobody noticed.

Or if they did notice, they just shrugged it off. Some people had probably hit the "sauce" before coming to the party.

Felicity staggered backward, rubbing the hand that had touched the non-Daniel. Jake caught her. She turned to me, eyes wide, looking a little green. I really hoped she had just stepped into one of the streams of colored light from the gels spotting the ceiling, and physical contact hadn't done something nasty to her. Kurt and Jane flickered out for a few seconds as they walked through the table and into the place where the fake Daniel had been standing. Hey, it was the fastest way to get to the scene of the crime before people walked through it and dissipated whatever clues the intruder, duplicate, whatever he was, might have left behind.

"What's wrong?" Daniel -- the real Daniel -- caught hold of my arm and went down on one knee so we were eye-level.

He had been doing that an awful lot lately. Touching my arm, my hand, going down on one knee to talk with me, and other little gestures, like stopping by for lunch every two or three days at the newspaper office. Things that had been giving me weird ideas.

"What's going on that we're getting invaded with no warnings, no dreams, no thrumming?" I said, instead of what had been in my head with such intensity I did feel a little queasy.

This was New Year's Eve. If the doppelganger had been sitting next to me when Kurt's super deluxe ball drop clock went off, would I have kissed him?

Oh.

Ugh.

Chapter Two

"Have you been getting any kind of feeling of being spied on? Something trying to latch onto your brain? Maybe ... I don't know ... sneaking around and borrowing pieces of your life?" I blurted.

Gagness -- that sounded like a bunch of B-grade movie plots.

I turned to Kurt and Jane. They were looking at the open floor between them and shaking their heads. I got ticked, because that doppelganger of Daniel, or whatever it or he was, had intruded on their really important moment. They turned to look at me and shrugged, and I interpreted that to mean they hadn't detected anything. Maybe the doppelganger was an illusion? But no, I tossed that theory aside as soon as it was clear in my head. Felicity had touched him, and she got some reaction in her hand. I turned to her, and she seemed to be fine. Jake would have carried her out of the gym by now if she had been hurt. They were huddled together, and she was smiling at him, probably to convince him she was fine.

Then the lights flashed through the gym and the band let out a clashing, crashing chord of sound and the ball drop clock burst into life. Five minutes until midnight Everyone in the room, other than at our table, let out a cheer as the countdown flashed across the screen. For the first four minutes, the LED numbers only changed every ten seconds. The last stragglers came racing back into the gym, alerted by the chords and flashing lights. Kurt had rigged things so the lights throughout the building flashed the warning that the countdown had begun. Just to make sure no one missed out on the stroke of midnight.

At one minute until midnight, the numbers changed at the fives.

Then at ten seconds, the official countdown began, with everyone in the gym chanting in unison.

Daniel tapped my arm and I nearly screamed. I turned my head in time to see Kurt go down on one knee in front of Jane again. Daniel grinned at me and reached for the bottle of sparkling cider on our table. I reached for Felicity and Mum, just as Pop joined us, and gestured at Kurt and Jane.

At "two," Kurt pulled a little ebony box from his pocket. I had seen that box at Divine's, and it appeared on the shelf of his workshop about three months after Jane came to town. Took him long enough to build up the courage. At midnight, when the countdown clock went cosmic and everyone shouted, "Happy New Year!" Kurt slipped it on her finger and stood up and they kissed. The rest of us turned our backs to give them a little bit of privacy.

Except for Daniel, who popped the top on the sparkling cider and slopped it into the plastic champagne flutes as fast as he could. Okay, the man did have a romantic streak.

Should I be scared?

~~~~~

The party was officially over for us, of course. The guardians of Neighborlee were back on duty, with that doppelganger sneaking up on us in the middle of the party. Kurt and Jane hadn't felt the power until they turned on the Ghost field for some invisibility and privacy. Then there was the question of whether the doppelganger had managed to hide its presence from the Hound, if it was tied into the Blues Brothers wannabes, or just an unhappy coincidence that it showed up when they did.

I hoped we could limit the impromptu conference to just those of us at the table who had experienced it, but of course, our numbers had grown in the last couple years. Once several of us were on alert, something like a subliminal message went out to the rest of us, guardians and support staff and allies alike.

Besides, Demetrius, Beau, Amelia, and other elders of Hoax were at the party, and they were waiting for Jane to show them that ring. When she didn't come running to them, they came looking for her, just in time to see the people from our table heading out of the gym. Ford sensed something wrong, and Athena and Wallace had been in on the whole proposal plan and were watching, so they came hurrying over as soon as everyone got up from our table.

I had really hoped we could sneak out without anyone noticing. Over the years, the guardians had basically learned to be posted near an exit, so we could leave quickly for impromptu meetings, or race out to whatever disaster had struck somewhere else. We had joked a few times over the last year about making business cards and calling ourselves the Avengers, except we
~~~~~

would have had to deal with copyright infringement. And more important, if we did fall into that storyline, eventually the world governments would have tried to make us sign agreements to only deal with emergencies they approved. And look how that worked out for Senator Ross and all the interfering self-righteous goons. I always wondered why Iron Man didn't have a bunch of reservations in mind when he snapped his fingers and brought everybody back from the blip. Why couldn't he have added, "except for the people who really were a pain in the neck and tried to tell us how to think"?

I digress. Because there were so many dang things filling my head during that short trip from our table, out the doors, and down the hall to the small gym where we had been playing Murder.

By the time Kurt got the lights turned on, we had quite a crowd of people who had followed us out. My whole family, which meant Meggie came along with Pete. All the Longfellows and the girls' boyfriends, Cosmo and Wallace. Holly and Maurice. Bethany and Harry. Brick and Lori. Dawn and Stanzer. Daniel's grandparents and parents. Demetrius, Beau, and a dozen other elders of Hoax who I hadn't been introduced to yet because they had arrived an hour into the party.

Wait. How could we be sure they really were members of Hoax and not some more doppelgangers?

"What?" Daniel said, this time leaning down from behind me, so his breath brushed my check. I felt his hands resting on the handles of my chair. Not so comforting right now, after all the images that had been dancing in my head.

Especially since I realized I had said some of what I had been thinking. That was not a good sign, thinking out loud.

"All the people who showed up late. How do we know --"

"That we aren't imposters?" Demetrius gave one of his dry coughing chuckles and sank down into one of the folding chairs that had been left up from the Morgue. "We've had some problems like that in the past, and we've designated various people to do regular checks on us when we're out in public. Even now that most of the Rivals have done themselves in and don't seem to be bothering us, well, it's smarter to stay vigilant and expect something equally as nasty to rise up to fill the gap. Nature abhors a vacuum and all that claptrap."

"We've learned over the years, from bad experiences, to send out an identification beep, something like bats' radar," Amelia said. "We know the feeling of each other's minds and our physical signs. And we've pretty much stayed together since we arrived. Being surrounded by strangers puts us on alert, anyway."

"So if you had sensed something odd, some note in the atmosphere," Angela said slowly, "you wouldn't have known if that was a threat or just being in an unfamiliar space?"

"Unfortunately, yes," Beau said. "Well, Cookie, what did you two sense, what did you flush out of hiding when you should have been otherwise ..." He waggled his bushy eyebrows.

I nearly burst out laughing at the sight of Jane blushing. Kurt grinned like an awkward teen and looked away. The way he caught hold of her hand, with the ring, and clutched it between both of his made me both happy and furious. Just for a few seconds. Because doggone it, we had a new troublesome problem and enemy to deal with, and it was interfering with their happy moment.

Because whatever had been masquerading as Daniel had reacted the way it did when its cover had been blown ... chances were good it hadn't been there just to crash a party.

There was magic involved, which meant interdimensional trouble.

We didn't come to any real conclusion once we had updated everyone on what had happened, and got their impressions of the evening, any twitches or glitches in the general atmosphere. We included my sighting of the Hound and what little Stanzer had been able to pick up. It wasn't really that comforting to know that the threat the Hound sensed had left the building. It hadn't been able to follow the strangers. The energy dissipated as soon as the badly dressed party crashers walked out the doors. Like they had faded away, just as the doppelganger of Daniel had done?

Not a pleasant thought.

Athena and Wallace got on their smartphones and contacted London and Sherwood, to see if our friendly, watchful AI's had noticed anything. Chances were they hadn't, because they would have tried to warn us. On the other hand, if this was the start of some nasty invasion, maybe the enemy knew about them monitoring the shield around our town and had done something to stop them from contacting us.

London popped up as soon as Athena contacted her. No interference, meaning she wasn't being prevented from communicating. That really wasn't a relief, because something or someone had the ability to keep our friendly AI's from noticing the invasion.

"Unless of course that thing has been inside the shield all along and is such an integral part of the weirdness of Neighborlee," Sherwood said, when he joined the conversation, "we wouldn't have noticed, because there wouldn't have been any change."

"Not even using power it hasn't been using before?" Ford said.

"What if it's been doing that all this time?" Pete said. He put his arm around Meggie, a defensive gesture I thought was sweet. Except he was frightening the rest of us with what he had thought of, which we should have thought of. Still, he was proving once again his value as a member of the support team. His massive, voracious reading of anything SF or fantasy provided him with a lot of material for theories and explanations. "What if there's been something running around town for years, pretending to be any of us, and this is just the first time it got caught?"

"Not a comforting thought," Pop said.

"Unless they're like Winkies," Maurice offered. "Always there, keeping watch, maybe even helping out, but most of the time just irritating and sparkling in the corner of your eye. Whenever you turn, they're not there, but you know something was there."

"I don't know if that's comforting or not," Angela said. Then she had to repeat what Maurice said for those who couldn't see or hear him.

"What if these doppelganger things have been part of what's been protecting us all these years?" Athena said, speaking slowly, her gaze unfocused. "When we were little kids, we had lots of make-believe friends, remember?" She turned to Bethany, who nodded. "What if they weren't make-believe? What if they were these doppelganger thingies, and only kids could see them, and just like with the Wishing Ball, the ones who stopped believing in magic stopped seeing them and ..." She sighed and shrugged. "It made more sense when it was kind of foggy in my head."

"No, makes a lot of sense." Wallace put his arm around her, squeezing her close. There was an awful lot of that going on tonight, which made sense, considering it was New Year's and we had just had another too-close encounter of the bizarre kind. "So we've had invisible helpers all these years, only now they're messing up? Or one of them just got tired of being invisible and decided to borrow Daniel's face so he could join in the fun?"

"Which begs the question why it chose Daniel, specifically." Kurt turned to me with that look I knew so very well. The protective big brother expression. "Maybe to get at Lanie?"

There is a big difference between everyone watching me when I'm on stage doing a comedy routine, and everybody looking at me when I'm not on stage. Especially when they get that worried, speculative look. Especially when they forget for a few seconds that even though I'm a broken semi-pseudo-superhero, I *am* a semi-pseudo-superhero, and I'm on the mend, and God gave me my somewhat unsatisfying powers for a reason and a purpose. For those few seconds, all people see is my wheelchair. It's enough to make me get up out of my chair and stomp over and punch someone and say, "Hey, stop looking at the wheels, look me in the face. My eyes are up here."

My legs were feeling that tingly-numb I hated, when I just knew they would start spazzing and shaking in another moment. The entire reason why, even though I knew I could walk, I didn't risk leaving my chair. Because my legs could fold on me at any second and send me falling flat on my face.

"Oh, heck," I groaned, and thumped my knees with my fists.

Yeah, my legs were tingly-numb. Which they *hadn't* been for nearly a year now, since a lot of the Rivals' interference and draining of Neighborlee's energy had been cut off or at least turned down in intensity. My legs had felt that sensation so rarely, I really should have noticed when it came back.

"Something's hinking with the defensive energy again," I said. "I've been so stressed about … about different things, I didn't notice when my legs started tingling and going spastic again."

"We're on it," London said. There was a flash from Athena and Wallace's smartphones, and our two AI's vanished.

"But why didn't they feel it?" Jane said. "And why didn't we?"

"If it's gradual," Angela said. "A little at a time, slowly, would we notice?"

"Like the frog in the pot of water on the stove," Ford said. "That's what got us in trouble in the first place. We didn't realize the energy was being drained away until we needed a big dose and we didn't have it." His gaze flicked over to Bethany, and then away again.

She didn't react, and I was glad, because I knew what Ford was thinking of. Stephanie, Bethany's mother, had been a fellow guardian. She had gone out in a torrential storm to deal with Big Ugly, and she had been so drained from her effort to patch the cracks in the dimensional gate, she had died. She shouldn't have, she wouldn't have, if the defensive energy surrounding Neighborlee hadn't been slowly drained away. The same energy should have healed my shattered back, and I never should have ended up in my wheelchair.

"Fool me once, shame on you," Angela murmured. "Fool me twice --"

"Ain't gonna happen," Kurt said. "We need to strike while there's any chance of that thing leaving a trail. Feel like going for a little moonlight flight?"

Before Felicity or I could respond, because our automatic assumption was that we were included when it came to flying, he and Jane flicked out.

"Never get used to them doing that," Ford muttered. "Angela, sometimes these kids really make me feel old."

She didn't respond, but her little smirk clearly said, "Speak for yourself, old man."

That light moment didn't last very long. We had to leave the small gym because there was a gang who wanted to play Murder to close down the party. They didn't know what had happened, and they at least had the right to bring in the new year with laughter.

"I think we need to do some big research," Pop said, when we had moved to a vacant classroom far down one wing of Eden, to ensure privacy. "If this is an instance of invisible guardians suddenly changing their routine, maybe their attitude and how they deal with the ordinary Humans under their care, there could be a pattern. Somewhere in history, in ancient cultures. We need to find that pattern. Or at least get a clue what we might be working with."

"I know I haven't been around very long," Dawn said. She was sitting with Athena, Doni, Bethany, and Meggie. "It just seems to me, from all I've been learning about Neighborlee, Angela is kind of the clearinghouse. The center of everything. So shouldn't these guardian spirits or whatever they are sort of, I don't know, report to her? So if she doesn't know about them, either there's something else going on, or they aren't guardian spirits or ... I don't know, something else is trying to move in and take over?" She flinched a little when I saw dawning apprehension on other faces, and suspected that look was on my face, too. "I'm probably twisting things out of shape, but, sorry, I've got invasion on my mind, what with Gahlmorag and all that."

"No, don't apologize," Angela said. "Harry, Lori, could you check with those who would know? I will of course contact Asmondius, but ... well, Maurice got me thinking, comparing this doppelganger or whatever it was with winkies. There are far more inimical forces in the other dimensions than even I am aware of, with all my years at my post."

"Could be a lot of political garbage going on," Maurice offered. "People finagling to get their own doorkeepers posted by making you look bad, making it look like there's a bigger threat to Neighborlee than there really is."

"Wouldn't put it past them," Bethany's Harry said, nodding.

"So like we've got the Fae gunning for us now? Maybe to take over the doorway that Neighborlee has been guarding all these years?" Felicity said.

"That's what we need to find out, either eliminate the possibilities or get more information for us to work on," Angela said.

So that was basically where we left things when we finally split up to go home and run the few errands we had agreed on, to send out questions and ask for information and report what had happened. Arthur Sheridan promised to have his people testing and questing and searching.

On the way home, by myself, I really kicked myself a few times for gloating just a few hours before over how I had my house all to myself again. I didn't want to be alone, which was kind of disturbing.

So it was a good thing I still wasn't asleep at 2:45am, working on my next *Talk to Terry* column, when London took over my computer screen to report in. She apologized for not recognizing that the lack of change in the energy filling Neighborlee over the holidays was actually a danger sign.

"Come again?" I wondered for a moment or two if I had fallen asleep and was dreaming this report.

"We should have gotten surges of energy from all the high holiday spirits and good will spilling into town from about Thanksgiving onward. There was a *slight* rise. Enough to make us think everything was fine. We should have realized the energy bubbles should have been a lot higher and stronger. Meaning something was draining that extra energy all the visitors and shoppers and holiday activities have brought into town."

"And with the big surge of excitement from New Year's, whatever happened when the doppelganger came into the party and masqueraded as Daniel … it was covered up?" I guessed.

Yeah, I had been reading some of the right science fiction books, but obviously not all, or not enough.

"Basically. We're tracking down its footprints, its energy signature. We think we've found one weak spot where it slipped through the defensive shield."

"So it came from outside?" That little bit of news gave me a jolt of energy. I was not going to bed any time soon.

"Looks like it."

"And it hasn't slithered out again," Sherwood reported, as my computer screen split in two to let him show up. "At least, as far as we can tell."

"So what's it doing? Who is it masquerading as and who is it bothering right --"

My doorbell rang. That freaked me out, because nobody ever used the doorbell. I only had a doorbell on the front door, and the only people who used it were people I didn't know. Why would a stranger be ringing my doorbell at nearly 3am on New Year's Day? My office window was on the back of the house, my blinds and curtains were down to block out the cold radiating through the glass, and there no lights on to let anyone know I was home or awake.

"Is something out there?" I asked, when the two AI's just blinked at me.

"I can't really … tell," London said after a pause that felt way too long for me. "We'll have to get back to you." The screen blanked, and for a second I had to fight down a sense of being abandoned.

My legs started aching and jerking, with those near-cramps that I could only deal with if I got up and walked around. I jerked myself up out of my wheelchair, and suddenly I got a freaky, stupid, nasty idea. I snatched up my phone from the side table where it was charging and unplugged it. As I walked, carefully, out of my office and aimed for the front door, I texted Kurt. Just in case whoever was outside had really sharp ears and could hear any conversations going on inside. Which might mean it heard what London and Sherwood and I had been discussing.

Something or someone at my door. How close are you?

By the time I got down the hall and turned to cut through the living room, my phone pinged.

Over the schools.

Knowing how Kurt and Jane could go near-sonic speeds in the Ghost field, they were probably over my house by the time I took five steps. Granted, my steps were really slow. I put my phone in my pocket, mentally shrugging as I realized I was in summer-weight pajamas and about to open my door to frigid temperatures. I paused to study the silhouette visible in the little porthole window of the front door. There were no lights on behind me. Not even the nightlight in the fan over the stove. That had burned out two weeks ago, and I had been too busy preparing for a full blow-out family Christmas to deal with things like replacing the bulb.

The enemy couldn't see me. Unless he could see through solid objects, and then the gig was up anyway.

Chapter Three

Another knock. Then a voice that sounded like Daniel called through the door, "Lanie? Are you okay? I'm pretty sure you aren't able to get to bed after all that weirdness." He laughed, and it was Daniel's laugh.

His normal laugh. Not the ragged, kind of awkward laugh he had been using the last few weeks.

The real Daniel would know that I couldn't sleep for all the ideas swirling through my head after what happened at Eden.

Right now, I was kind of hoping Daniel was at the door. Maybe we could finally have some privacy to discuss things, like why he couldn't seem to look me in the eye lately, or make jokes, and why he kept on the other side of the room during our Star Trek club Christmas party.

I wiped my suddenly sweaty hands on my pants. Oh, yeah, I was in my pajamas. I didn't want Daniel to see me dressed like this. Besides, why would he come at nearly 3am? Why would he use the front door? He had always used the kitchen door, from the very first time he came to my house.

Proof he wasn't Daniel? Kind of a relief ... Still, opening it to the doppelganger wasn't very smart, either. Then I looked down at my legs again. I was standing up. The reaction of whichever Daniel was at the door would clarify who he was. Besides, Kurt and Jane were probably hovering --

My phone pinged, as if he heard my thoughts.

Here. Did you know Daniel glows in the dark?

Duh. Not him.

Plan?

Pincer move? Get ready.

I took the last few steps to the door. My knees wobbled. Too much time standing, and I didn't note when I got up, so I didn't know if my upright-on-my-own-feet-again time was increasing. I winced as I hit the light switch next to the door, fearing I would hit the wrong one of the three. One switch for the light outside, one for directly over the door inside, and another light at the other end of the room. Like I said before, we never used the front door. Which should have been proof enough whoever was there wasn't Daniel. So did the doppelganger glow because Kurt and Jane saw it through the Ghost field?

Taking a deep breath, I flipped the deadbolt and yanked hard to pull the door open. It stuck -- because, hey, never used -- and groaned as I pulled it open.

Daniel grinned at me and reached for the screen door handle.

He glowed, an odd, black light sort of effect, like when dead Obi-Wan showed up to talk to Luke. Or Bob Newhart as Professor Proton talked to Sheldon, much against his will. Professor Proton, not Sheldon.

"Hey, I knew you'd be up." Doppelganger Daniel frowned at the screen door that didn't cooperate when he tried to pull it open. "You gonna let me in? We really need to talk."

"The Bible says not to welcome malevolent spirits," I said, and stepped back, crossing my arms. That wasn't exactly what the Bible said, but since the devil twisted it all the time, whoever this guy was couldn't exactly fault me. Besides, the Bible did teach not to welcome opposing forces. Kind of along the lines of not letting vampires into your house. Once they got in, they could always get in, and rescinding the welcome was hard. Usually because by the time someone figured out they had made a mistake, they were dead. Or un-dead, depending on the vampire universe.

"Mal -- what?" He grinned. Definitely not Daniel. The real Daniel would understand that word, and the implications.

Really, what more proof did I need?

And still this thing looked at me and didn't react to me being on my own two feet. Which were getting kind of achy. So was this a different doppelganger? Or didn't he notice I was sitting in a wheelchair when he planted himself next to me at our table at the party less than three hours ago?

"Hey, a little help here!" I shoved hard with my mind.

I was half afraid my telekinetic fist would go right through the doppelganger, but to my great satisfaction, he went flying off the front step and out into the snow with a satisfying *ooph*, wide-eyed and stunned. The black light effect flared and shot off crackles of static and sparks before dropping back to its starting levels.

Kurt and Jane stepped out of a slit in the air. They also hovered about two feet above the top of the snow drifts.

Doppelganger Daniel scrambled backward in the snow for a few feet. It was more than a foot deep, because hey, I never used the front door. The mailbox was on the side of the house, so brother Harry never shoveled the front sidewalk. Come to think of it ... I looked in the last of the fading black light streaks, and there were no footprints leading up to my front door.

"The thing teleports or whatever. It didn't walk here," I called out, as Kurt and Jane split up to perform their pincer move on the doppelganger as it struggled to its feet.

"What do you want?" Kurt spread his arms.

Jane mirrored him. Swirls of light radiated out from their hands and spun around, forming a sphere around the melting thing that no longer looked like Daniel. Kind of gross, but nothing like the melting wax figures they used in the opening-the-Ark-and-creating-chaos scene from *Raiders of the Lost Ark*.

It made little squawking noises, then sort of flattened and slid sideways, shooting off a cascade of fractured, dirty-looking light as the walls of the Ghost field squeezed it. Too late. It flared, more ugly black light special effects, and sped across the yard. Through the snow fence the Mulcahys put up next door. Out into the street. Through four cars. Then vanished from sight, leaving streaks of red light behind it.

Kurt and Jane sped after it, joining hands a second before they vanished, enclosed by the Ghost field. I stood there long enough the cold air through the screen door penetrated my pajamas. My shivering combined with my wobbling knees and aching feet and tired thighs to send me sliding down the frame of the door to the floor. Real good.

I scooted back away from the door far enough to shove it closed with my mind. That kind of hurt, meaning my mental punch to the doppelganger took a lot more energy than I intended. I got up onto my knees enough to flip the light switch and got the door locked again. Then I sagged back against the wall to catch my breath.

Okay, I was on the floor in the living room. My options were to crawl to the kitchen, where I could pull myself up and navigate by holding onto chairs and counters. That made sense to me, because I was going to need to chow down on something before my reaction headache hit. Best bet was chocolate milk and trail mix, and then those to-die-for treats Jane and Felicity and Holly and I had created when we were goofing around a week ago. Little Debbie oatmeal cream pies, sandwiched together with peanut butter, dipped in melted chocolate.

And why was I sitting there, thinking about food, when I should be getting into the kitchen before my head started throbbing and my stomach clenched so tightly I couldn't move for the cramps?

I went on my hands and knees. Not as bad as I had feared. I got into the kitchen and pulled myself up by holding onto the closest chair. I was slightly out of breath and fighting a little vertigo, which worried me, when my phone rang. I nearly burst into tears when I saw the call was from Mum. That told me more clearly than my shaking legs and aching head that I had really strained myself with that doppelganger.

"What happened?" Mum demanded, before I finished saying hello.

"The doppelganger showed up here. Kurt and Jane chased it. They're still chasing it, as far as I know."

In the background, as she repeated what I had just said, I heard the grumble of the trusty old VW minibus that had been old when Mum and Pop adopted me.

"We saw something, but we didn't know what it was, too much light, too much warping."

"How?" I aimed myself for the refrigerator. The spikes in my temples needed a good dose of chocolate milk before they got any deeper and met up with the corkscrew aching sensation coming up through my stomach.

"We went back to Divine's with Angela and Maurice and Holly, to talk." Mum sighed. "And see if there was anything we could find in some of those very esoteric books she keeps locked up. Angela and I both got a feeling that something was wrong with you. Maurice persuaded the Wishing Ball to show us what was happening. There was a figure in your doorway and -- Lanie, why did you open the door?"

"It couldn't get in. It needed me to let it in." I nearly laughed as I realized what had happened. It really was like in the rules laid down by *Buffy*: vampires can't get in where they aren't welcome. The doppelganger had gone right through the fence and those cars, but *couldn't* get into my house ... because I hadn't welcomed it or invited it in. "Where are you?"

"We're about to turn into your neighborhood."

"Okay, let me pull out supplies for a long talk. I really need to get off my feet. The back door's open."

Mum let me get off the phone. I barely remembered to flip the locks on the back door before I tottered over to the refrigerator. And then I drank straight from the jug. I didn't care that I spilled a few drops of chocolate milk on my shirt. Mopping up those dribbles made me aware once again I was in my summer-weight pajamas. The ones with worn thin spots that were fine when it was just all girls, but it wasn't just my parents coming to check on me. Besides, Kurt and Jane would come back as soon as they finished dealing with the doppelganger.

Maybe I should be worried, the longer it took them to come back?

I snagged my big, fluffy red robe and slippers. My feet were cold, too. I put water in the coffeemaker, to brew up some of Pop's special recipe tea, and I was pulling all sorts of treats out of the cupboards when the back door opened. Mum and Angela led the way. Holly was behind them. Maurice leaped off her shoulder, out from under her fluffy scarf, and zipped around the kitchen before coming to hover in front of me.

"You okay, kiddo?" He looked me up and down, eyebrows rising as he looked at my legs. I was standing up, but more leaning on the counter than really standing. It was the only way I could reach the shelves where I had stashed the really good homemade goodies. Starting with those deluxe oatmeal cream pies.

I shrugged. I wasn't about to admit that his reaction to seeing me on my feet, when he knew I was starting to get my legs back, was a little more reassuring than was good for me. The doppelganger hadn't reacted at all. Did that mean it knew my legs were coming back, or the doppelganger just didn't know me well enough, or didn't notice enough details to wonder?

"Here, let me do that." Angela gently but firmly shoved me back down into my wheelchair, which I had had the sense to get and bring into the kitchen. She and Mum bustled around the kitchen, bringing out cups and plates and putting the containers of goodies I indicated on the table.

By that time, Pop had come in, stomping snow off his boots. Considering my driveway and the backyard had been shoveled clean, that meant he had been walking around the house, examining the scene of the doppelganger's mad scramble to get away from Kurt and Jane.

Maurice flew into the living room and did something. From where I was sitting, I could see him flying back and forth across the front door, up and down, diagonally. He never tried to open the door, but he must have found out something, because he was scowling when he came back into the kitchen and got close enough I could see his face. A head less than an inch tall didn't really reveal much detail until he was nearly up to my nose.

"You got glowing streaks in the air, going around the house," Pop reported, once he had hung up his coat and pried off his boots. "I don't think ordinary eyes can see it, but ever since last summer, I can kind of squint and see things." He shrugged. "What's weird is the lack of footprints, except where it looks like something had a wrestling match for a few seconds."

"What did you see on the front door?" I asked Maurice.

"Something was trying to get in." He shook his head and stomped across the table to the doll-sized table and beanbag chair I kept on hand for when he visited. All the plastic Barbie-style furniture wasn't very comfortable. "There were fingerprints or whatever all around the frame, and along the walls, like it was trying to ooze through but couldn't find a hole. What's really weird is there is no energy, no magic keeping anything out. Unless your really good construction and insulation works against spookies like they work against bugs and weather."

"Nothing you can *sense*," Angela gently corrected him. "Whatever this thing is, it seems to obey certain ancient protocols … which still doesn't seem to help us identify it."

"Kurt and Jane are chasing it. Maybe they'll find out some things to help us," I said.

"Okay, honey, what happened?" Pop picked up the carafe of tea now that the coffeemaker had finished brewing, and brought it over to the table.

Telling about the little encounter didn't take very long. Taking it apart detail by detail and speculating and comparing with old folk tales and things Maurice could remember from lessons in his childhood took us the next three hours. I knew Mum and Pop wanted to ask Maurice about the kind of lessons a Fae child would have to learn, and anything he could share about the Fae Realms equivalent of the boogieman. They just made little notes in their ever-present notebooks and kept the conversation on the topic of my particular boogieman.

Angela was unusually silent, meaning either she didn't have any information to add, or she felt now was not the right time to tell us what she did know. Or maybe she needed to do more research. We were discussing the whole vampire concept of being unable to enter without a welcome when Kurt and Jane came back. They had something interesting to add, and just reignited the whole oogie sensation in my gut all over again.

They had been inside the Ghost field when I gave the doppelganger a hard mental punch in the chest. That spot where I hit it had given off a purplish glow among the red trail of energy the doppelganger left behind when it fled. As they chased it, the purple faded to green and then brown, like a bruise. As the colors changed, and going by the analogy of a bruise, as the doppelganger healed, it moved faster. Kurt and Jane had stayed back, just keeping it in sight, hoping it would lead them to its nest -- bad mental image -- or to the place where it had come through into Neighborlee.

"When it first ran away, it went in a straight line for the nearest border," Kurt reported. He reached for the deluxe oatmeal cream pie he had been eyeing since he and Jane sat down at the table. "What?" he said, when she and I exchanged grins. "Is there a boobytrap or something hidden inside? Something only girls are supposed to like eating?"

"It's a recipe we came up with," I said. "We're just curious if you'll like it, that's all."

"Uh huh." He glanced between us a few times, then opened his mouth as wide as it could go and took a bite. He closed his eyes and chewed a few times. Paused. Opened his eyes. Turned the pie over a few times, examining it. Then chewed a half dozen more times, before taking a swig of tea to wash it down. "Umm, Jane ... did I ask you to marry me yet?"

"Changing your mind?" She leaned back in her seat, shoulders shaking slightly from repressed laughter.

"Heck no! This would just seal the deal if I hadn't made up my mind already."

The rest of us laughed, and Kurt nearly inhaled the oatmeal pie. Too soon, though, the light moment passed. He returned to what he had been saying.

"The freaky thing is, it hit the line where Neighborlee met Cutterville and it bounced back. There was a flare, a color of light or energy I've never seen before." He shook his head, contemplating his empty mug for a moment. "It seemed like there was a matching flare on its body where it hit, around the shoulders and upper arm, like if a linebacker tried to bulldoze through a defending line. That flare faded when it backed up and changed its angle. Then it hit the shield again and bounced back even farther than the first time."

"We've spent most of the last few hours following it around, staying on the Neighborlee side of the border with the surrounding towns," Jane said. "Each time, the same flare of some kind of energy we've never seen before, and that flash of bruised light where it ran into the shield. Each time, it waited until the bruise faded to brown before it tried again. The whole thing was starting to feel a little frantic near the end."

"Yeah, I could almost feel sorry for it," Kurt said, through a mouthful of his second oatmeal pie. "The weird thing is that I was pretty sure it couldn't see us or even sense us, hidden in the Ghost field. But that was the only way we could see it. We experimented about an hour ago." He checked his watch and nodded. "Yeah, just short of an hour ago. We stepped out of the field, and the thing vanished. We brought up the field again and there it was, trying to get over the border into Darbyville. It slammed against the shield five or six times before it gave up and ran away."

"And all this time, did it still look like Daniel, or did it take on its real face or shape or whatever?" Pop asked.

Good one. I hadn't even thought about that aspect of the doppelganger problem.

"Not really sure," Jane said after a few moments when she and Kurt wore almost matching frowns of concentration. "It was just a shape. Like a silhouette against all that rippling light that wasn't exactly black light, but not really any color at all."

"A man shape, yeah," Kurt said. "Maybe it got thicker than

Daniel, and taller, but definitely a man, as opposed to a woman or a kid."

"I'm sorry," Pop said, "but I have the feeling none of the books in our library really cover something this or even offer hints. Angela, we might be camping at your place for the duration."

"I would be disappointed if you didn't pursue this," Angela said. "Whether this is a new enemy or puzzle, or simply a new face or ploy by Big Ugly or this Kerri woman ... we need answers if we are to properly fight it. What disturbs me is that the creature seems trapped inside our borders."

"Nope." Kurt shook his head, giving us a grim little smile. "If it was still here on our turf, we'd still be tailing it and taking notes."

"So what happened?" Maurice asked. "It imploded? Or it escaped?"

"We're not really sure," Jane said, after the two of them exchanged those looks that always implied compressed communication. "About ten minutes after that experiment of becoming visible to it again, it came to a place where we could *see* the shield. It was sort of glowing, just for a few seconds, but getting stronger as the doppelganger approached it. Again, no color we could recognize."

"And when it leaped, it got through?" I guessed.

"The creepy thing sort of flashed and this spiderweb of really ugly, dirty light spread out from the spot where it hit the barrier," Kurt said. "Then it was gone. If it blew up or it got through the shield, who knows? We had no trouble crossing the border and we flew up and down along the general area, looking for signs. No more trail of bruised light, no footprints in the snow, no humming feeling. Nothing."

"Weren't the kids doing something with the shield?" Pop asked after several minutes of everyone around the table looking thoughtful. "I mean, yeah, it's a little embarrassing to realize that this shield we've talked about around our town for years is real, know what I mean? We've kind of sidestepped it, almost joking about it, but now to realize that yes, there is a dividing line, and it's been protecting us, or not protecting us because it's been sabotaged ..." He shook his head. "So if the kids have been monitoring it, checking out its health or whatever, maybe they felt something?"

Maybe I was finally tired, but it took me until he finished

talking to realize Pop meant London and Sherwood. And what he was saying made a lot of sense.

We got a few more surprises when Kurt stepped into my office to get my tablet, so we could contact our friendly AI's with a screen all of us at the table could look at. We discovered Sherwood had been pinging me. And hadn't been able to ping Kurt and Jane.

That was the second or maybe third or fourth weird discovery of the night. Actually, morning, since dawn was heading our way a lot sooner than any of us anticipated. The short explanation for what Sherwood had discovered was that something had hinked up our phone signals. London had established a very light touch on all our electronic gizmos way back when Freddie Grandstone was trying to romance Athena into servitude to the Rivals. This was so she could always know where we were, and she didn't have to fight any natural electronic interference that might be in the area if she needed to communicate.

However, something had effectively closed a heavy door on the signals for our three phones. The link still functioned, just strong enough to know we were there, but nothing could get through. My signal had cut off when I went to the door to confront the doppelganger. Kurt and Jane's phone links got squeezed, or maybe strangled would be a more appropriate word, when they crossed the border, in their effort to follow the doppelganger.

"So how do we get it back?" Kurt put his phone down on the table next to my tablet, where Sherwood's image gave a very good impression of a sleepless night.

"We're working on it." He glanced off-screen, which really wasn't necessary, since he wasn't physically anywhere.

Just to show how my brain was starting to fog up and not all the cylinders were firing in synch, I wondered just how many mannerisms London and Sherwood had picked up from us. Was it conscious? Was it deliberate mimicry? Was it something they couldn't control, and they were becoming more like their models, Doni and Cosmo, every day?

The screen split and London appeared in the right half. She was wearing her favorite outfit of black Greek fisherman's cap, black sweater and multiple fine silver chains. Actually, that was Athena's favorite outfit about a year ago. So what did that say about the AI's mimicry?

Yeah, I really needed to get horizontal and turn off the lights before my brain entirely imploded. I was getting sidetracked a little too easily.

"You all picked up a signal that's sort of like a parasitic vine," London reported. "It's weak, mostly just sucking at power right now, but we're worried that it's trying to wear down your security programs and get at vital information."

"Fortunately, you beefed up our security so nothing short of another artificial intelligence can get through. Right?" Kurt said. He sounded a little tense. Yeah, I could understand why. Tonight should have been romantic and entirely focused on him and Jane.

"Hey, I'm not exactly a fan of all this high-tech stuff," Maurice said, waving his arms. "Seems to me even on a lot of those shows the guys love, with all the computers and spaceships and such, the simplest fix is to just shut everything down and reboot, right?"

We all sat very still for about five seconds. Then London laughed. She nodded and held up her hand for a high five. Maurice flew over to the tablet and slapped at the screen. Less than a minute later, we had shut down our three phones, Sherwood verified the leach signal had vanished within ten seconds, we turned our phones back on, and everything was back to normal.

"Okay, so somebody is on the outside, tampering with the shield again?" Jane said.

"Looks like it," Sherwood said. "We were focusing on the shield, playing with some of our modulation programs, after Pete and Meggie saw something on an episode of *Stargate*. We've set up a pattern that doesn't repeat until nearly 500 modulations of the frequency. That's kind of taking up more of our attention than we anticipated." He shrugged. "Sorry."

"Something got lucky and squeezed through during an ultra-low dip," London said, taking up the explanation from him. "The energy signature matches whatever was bouncing off the shield on the Neighborlee side for more than two hours." She winced a little. "During a matching ultra-low dip in the modulation."

"We've altered the program so it doesn't go that low again," Sherwood hurried to add.

"So it couldn't get out -- that's what it was doing the whole time we were chasing it?" Kurt said. "Bouncing off the inside of the shield, trying to find a weak spot or low point?"

"And something else, either a partner or another entity like the doppelganger, was waiting and trying to penetrate the shield, and latched onto your phones when you flew out," she said.

"Why not another enemy altogether?" Maurice shrugged. "Sorry to be the downer in this war council, but you gotta consider the possibility."

"He's right," Angela said, "but that leach signal that latched onto Lanie's phone also caught onto Kurt and Jane's, correct?"

That was true, and we tried to see it as a positive -- we only had one enemy to deal with. Of course, we weren't sure how large the team was now attacking us, but that had to be better than facing enemies on two fronts, right?

So now we had to determine if the doppelganger was something new. Maybe another enemy had decided to make a move since Big Ugly had been seriously handicapped when he gulped down a whole bunch of Rival minions and whatever poison they were trying to pump into Eden. Talk about bad indigestion. Or maybe the doppelganger was just another face of the returning enemy that most recently had struck at us through the vampish Kerri, she of pale hair and skin, and black clothes.

All in all, not a good way to bring in the new year.

Especially when London and Sherwood informed us that with the energy signature of the doppelganger Kurt and Jane had dealt with, they had been able to backtrack all the tiny blips in the defensive field of Neighborlee. They had tracked down the place and time when the doppelganger got inside. Accessing a traffic camera on the Cutterville side of the intersection, they had identified Daniel's car crossing the border. So the next question was if the doppelganger had imprinted on Daniel, so it was stuck wearing his face when it tried to infiltrate the party at Eden. If so, did that mean it would always wear his face when it attacked, if it ever attacked again?

Chapter Four

Was it just a coincidence? Or was this a very recent development, maybe a new weapon in our enemy's arsenal? Arthur Sheridan came up with another theory when we presented the information to him much later that day: the doppelganger had been there for quite a while, hanging around Daniel since Sylvia Grandstone started her campaign to sink her claws into him. Yeah, it was a knee-jerk reaction to blame everything on the Rivals and their seeming generations of attacks on the secrets and strengths of our town. If the doppelganger had attached itself to Daniel, did that make him a weak spot in our combined forces? Maybe a liability?

Not very encouraging. Not a very nice way to start the new year, either. At least we waited until we had a lot more information from our friendly AI's, and we let everyone catch up on some desperately needed sleep before we hit them with the new challenge and danger of the new year.

Well, we were getting together anyway at the Sheridan house. Demetrius, Beau and Amelia were guests there, and we had an informal alliance conference planned. Assessing what we had done in the past year -- lots! Looking ahead to what we could attempt. Discussing what we hoped to learn from the latest Rivals depot our combined forces had uncovered and were still investigating. And yeah, celebrate that we had survived and triumphed against another attempt to infiltrate and take over our town.

Maybe we had celebrated too soon?

Maybe this was that quiet moment near the end of a horror movie, where there are only two or maybe three survivors, and they think they're home free. The open door and escape are only steps away. They smile and stumble and are ready to let out sighs of relief. And then the floor cracks open and something worse than all the other things they faced in the previous hour and forty-five minutes of movie, combined, rises up to launch at them.

We all got at least four hours of sleep between our pre-dawn meeting and heading over to Sheridans to take the gloss off their new year, too. That helped a little, or at least we were all thinking a little clearer. The important thing was to get everyone together and their various and assorted gizmos out, so London and Sherwood could scan them, de-bug if any kind of leach field was trying to dig its metaphorical teeth in, and upload a new defensive layer to our tech.

One fun little detail popped up. (Yes, speaking sarcastically.) Sherwood had detected a slight trace signal from both the doppelganger and whatever had latched onto Kurt and Jane's phones when they went through the shield. The trace signal died as soon as we turned our phones off, but there had been a sort of regular pulse or ping, trying to regain the signal, up until dawn. The moment the sun peeked over the horizon and light touched the place where the doppelganger had left Neighborlee air space, the ping died completely. London, Athena, Wallace, and Cosmo had been tag-team working on trying to track the source of the ping up until that point. Nice to know the younger members of the guardians' support squadron had given up their New Year's sleep to dive in and help, but it was essentially wasted effort. Nothing that an automatic monitoring program couldn't have found without their oversight and guidance.

Kind of depressing.

So we talked about our new or possibly old enemies being at least part vampire, unable to function in the full light of day. Like that didn't make it more scary than it had already been?

The upshot of the meeting was that Daniel went back to Hoax headquarters with Demetrius and Beau to be thoroughly examined. We needed to be sure something hadn't been planted on him, offering the as-yet-to-be-identified enemy a foothold of sorts. His general immunity to nasty, otherworldly attacks and power fields didn't guarantee he couldn't be invaded some way or another. It was something like the defensive shields in the first *Dune* movie, with all the crystalline special effects surrounding the fighters. Fast moves and powerful blows bounced off, but a slow-moving knife could penetrate all that high-tech defense. It just took patience and strength.

Whoever our enemies were now, whether old ones returning or new ones taking up where the last creeps left off, they were definitely patient, and if we were really unlucky, they had learned from the mistakes of their predecessors.

Yeah, Happy New Year.

~~~~~

Over the next few days, Sherwood notified us of several "collisions" with the shield. None of them were related to Neighborlee residents going in and out of town and crossing the borders. None of them coincided with people who lived in other towns and worked in Neighborlee, going in and out. We had no way of knowing if any more doppelgangers managed to hitch rides with people and to evade detection. Sherwood admitted that he and London were constantly playing with the connections they had forged between themselves and the energy that protected us and fed us, to monitor the fluctuations and feed the levels, and keep the fluctuations going at unpredictable non-patterns. They also tried to set up a resonance that vibrated inward from the shield, to try to determine if and when anything unfriendly managed to penetrate.

Just to be safe, we asked everyone on the team, whether Sheridan people or guardians or relatives or Hoax members who had come for an extended stay, not to go through the shield. Basically, not leave town. Just for a few days, to establish a pattern outside and inside for the natural energy flow from land and air and water and the life force "sea" on both sides.

Then on Tuesday, we conducted an experiment. Or rather, London contacted Dawn and Stanzer, and with the help of Athena and Wallace, conducted an experiment.

They went for a hike, staying inside the borders of Neighborlee, and walked along the border. When they got to the street where the line between Darbyville and our town went down the double yellow line -- yeah, that street, with the weird house that had tried to drain Angela all those years ago -- four Hounds appeared with an audible crackle of thunder, and blue lightning sizzling all over their coats. They put themselves between Dawn and Stanzer and that house, blocking them from view, and glared. At the house, fortunately, not Dawn and Stanzer.

Athena and Wallace later said they were going nuts, recording all the energy spikes and drops and swirls. Don't ask me what energy swirls were, other than an electronic version of a hurricane. All the craziness went off in response to the presence of two members of the Hunt and started before the Hounds showed up,
~~~~~

and sat down on the double yellow line. As soon as the guardian beasts did that, there was a huge spike in the energy and then it just dropped, like falling into a hole. In seconds, it was gone. Like nothing had happened.

Except the Hounds sat there and stared and growled at that troublemaking house for another ten, fifteen minutes. Dawn, Stanzer, Athena and Wallace retreated to the sidewalk and waited. And hoped very hard that no one was home in any of those houses, to call the police and complain about loiterers or accuse them of doing something illegal, or at least creepy.

The only conclusion we could come to was that someone or something hiding in that house recognized Dawn and Stanzer, and reacted in a way that the Hounds considered a threat. Bad enough to make them come zapping in from whatever sideways or parallel dimension they lived in when they weren't visible and doing their guard duty.

~~~~~

Athena and Wallace stopped in at the *Tattler* that Wednesday to talk with Monroe, our staff photographer. He was a classmate from WBC and was starting a side business doing portraits and wedding photography. They wanted to talk to him about both, because they had finally set the date, and were going to put the official engagement announcement in the paper.

Times like these made me feel really old. I remembered when Athena first came to Neighborlee, with those big, dark eyes watching everything and everyone. She wasn't the chubby, happy, constantly laughing baby that Bethany had been, but she struck me as peaceful. At least, until she got her feet under herself, and then she was constantly running in and out and around. Come to think of it, she was a lot like Pete had been as a baby. But the bottom line was, I remembered Athena as a baby, and now she was getting married. Even though they had just met during the gap between Thanksgiving and Christmas, Bethany and Harry the Fae (to differentiate from my brother Harry) were very good together and were probably heading for the altar too. My little girls were grown up. Stephanie would be so proud of her daughter. Although she might not have been so happy over Bethany discovering her mixed heritage of Fae and guardian, and all the implications that came with whatever was born into her blood.
~~~~~

Athena and Wallace had to wait a while, because Monroe hadn't come back yet from a photo shoot at the Browns training center. It was pretty quiet since Wednesday was a between-papers day, so the three of us were relaxing and talking. Other than Conrad in his office, and some of the circulation guys at the other end of the building, we pretty much had the place to ourselves. Matilda was busy at the copy machine, which provided enough acoustic coverage she wouldn't have heard us if we talked at the top of our voices. She wouldn't have cared if we had talked about the latest weirdness we had been dealing with.

We could have been talking about the shield and doppelganger situation. Instead, we were making plans for our next Trek club meeting. Harry and Lori both wanted to attend. That made sense, since Bethany wanted to reunite with the gang, and Brick Willis was a big part of the club, when he had time. Their new sweethearts wanted to learn more about their lives, as well as the whole living as a Human experience.

We were lucky we were so alone, because London woke up my computer and flashed onto my screen. She had just harvested news reports from Los Angeles. All about Bethany.

The really frightening part? There were six of them so far, and the alerts she had set up to keep track of Bethany and other Neighborlee natives living in the "outside world" didn't seem to be working like they should. Who could interfere with an AI's programming like that?

The most recent news feature was from a newspaper, rather than social media postings and YouTube videos, which might explain how that had triggered her alerts, while the others had been blocked or hidden.

"Doppelgangers again," Wallace muttered, after we had crowded together to read the articles on my screen. It was a good thing Conrad believed in the jumbo-sized computer monitors for all the staff writers. We needed the room.

All the stories dealt, in one way or another, with a lookalike of Bethany who was running around Hollywood, generating attention, treating her fans rudely, and getting into trouble. That is, until someone who knew Bethany got close enough or saw enough of the lookalike's actions, heard enough of her voice and her words, to declare her a fake. Each time, the fake's mannerisms changed, along with her voice, the moment she was outed. It took three recorded sightings and encounters before people noticed that the lookalike wore the same clothes each time. Now there was talk of a "spot the fake Bethany" game going around, where facial recognition software and similar programs were being used to find that specific outfit, track the imposter, and reveal her before she struck again. Before another overly enthusiastic Bethany Miller fan had an unpleasant encounter.

"Do you know where Bethany is?" I asked, as soon as we finished reading.

"Probably with Angela, getting guardian history lessons, or maybe talking with one of Harry's relatives. Maybe even that Asmondius guy," Athena said after a few seconds of thought.

"Why?"

"Gene therapy." She shrugged. "Bethany isn't anywhere near deciding if she wants to activate whatever is recessive Fae in her, but she wants to know about the process and what it means for her. Got the feeling she's really, really serious about Harry?"

"Hey," Wallace said, "when you find the right one, you lock her in and don't let go. Or him, as the case may be. I understand completely."

"He's so romantic," she muttered, rolling her eyes. But she blushed when Wallace hooked his arm around her waist and drew her up against his side, and smeared a big, noisy kiss on her check.

"We need to warn Bethany," I said, trying to ignore their foolery. "I'm surprised her agent hasn't been keeping her updated. Or her manager, or whoever is supposed to be looking out for her interests."

When we caught up with Bethany at Divine's Emporium, we found out her agent had been keeping her updated, just not on all the incidents. He had notified her after the third, when it started looking like a pattern was developing. Then right after he sent her an email with links to the YouTube and Facebook postings, with all the comments defending or vilifying Bethany, the fourth incident occurred. Bethany and everyone involved in her career needed to get to work. Things had turned serious. Yeah, as if they weren't already?

Her lookalike had appeared at the studio for the Nickelodeon series she regularly guest-starred in. The lookalike got through the studio gates and security system without setting off any blips. Bethany's agent was working on finding out how that happened, and why or how the security equipment had gone on the fritz the entire time the lookalike was on the property.

That frightening little side note made the six of us -- Angela, Bethany, Harry, Athena, Wallace and me -- pause and just look at each other for a few seconds.

The agent was worried. So far the nasty lookalike had made enough sloppy mistakes to easily reveal herself as an imposter. What was to halt the destruction of Bethany's career and her reputation if the imposter learned to pass herself off as the genuine article? Nickelodeon and the production company were already leery of getting caught up in the pointing fingers and accusations and all the ugliness that could ensue when fans suddenly turned on Bethany. When would they stop believing in the face she had been showing all these years, and decide the new, ugly Bethany was the real one?

"What happens when the lookalike goes after Bethany, to erase her so she can take over her life?" Wallace said.

"Not going to happen." Harry gripped Bethany's shoulders. The two of them partially phased out, turning into Bethany and Harry-shaped clouds of smoke.

"It can have my career." Bethany tried to smile. "I have to wonder if all this weirdness is a lot bigger than social media has figured out. I'm supposed to be heading back to L.A. for some meetings and casting interviews. My agent was supposed to send me a few scripts to look over, but he's gotten calls from the production companies saying to wait. Two meetings were canceled this morning. The Nickelodeon series has four scripts with my character, and just since the trouble started Monday afternoon, they've all been put on hold. All I need is one more good reason not to go back to Hollywood ever."

That reason came that evening. Well, Wednesday night in California, but the early morning hours of Thursday in Neighborlee.

Someone tried to break into Bethany's apartment. *Tried* being the operative word. They were stopped by the same protective Fae who had kept Bethany under observation since she was a baby, in case her father's diluted Fae heritage erupted into inconvenient life.

Those watchers had come to like Bethany, after seeing her at her worst and best. They were protective of her cozy little apartment because they knew it was her haven from the insanity of her career. They didn't like it when someone tried to break in. And when the intruder failed to pick the lock on her apartment door, then her balcony door, then the window of her bathroom, it tried to pry open the vent cover and slither down into her apartment.

The really serious Fae defenses kicked in, triggering an equal and vicious response from the creature trying to break in.

I say "creature" and "it" because Asmondius, when he reported what had happened to Angela, got a tight note in his voice and a curl in his upper lip, and referred to the invader as "it."

The resulting short battle with the defending Fae triggered alarms of the Human variety. The security cameras in the building and several stalker-type fans watching Bethany's building, waiting for her to return from vacation, all got pictures of *something*. Fae magic was at work overtime, because all the images were blurry, showing what looked like a person clinging to the window of Bethany's fourth floor apartment, trying to break in. Then slipping over to the balcony railing and beating on the sliding door. Meanwhile, lights flashed and sirens wailed and some cranky neighbor on the ground floor got hold of a maintenance team hose that had been left lying around and turned water on the intruder.

At which time it lost its grip and fell and nearly landed on the guy with the hose. All of which was caught on video cameras of various types. Building security and the police wanted to keep it quiet while they investigated, but the stalker fans posted it within ten minutes of the whole incident. There was some uproar in the papers and among the maintenance staff over that hose in the videos. When the staff person who should have put the hose away got reamed for it, he went over to the storage shed were all the lawn care equipment was kept and showed them the hose, neatly coiled up where it belonged, and dry. No hose could be found on that side of the building, and no sign of late-night watering. And yet the video showed the crazy neighbor with the hose and water spraying and the intruder falling.

To make matters worse, I had had a really bad dream while this was happening. I'm talking frightening images of something that looked like Bethany, but all warped and sort of melting around the edges, breaking into her apartment and yanking her out through the shattered balcony door. I had picked up on the attacker's *intentions*, since obviously Bethany wasn't there. I called Angela and she told me she was getting a report right that moment, and it might be smart to get Bethany and bring her to the shop, to hear what was going on. I picked up Bethany, Harry, and Ben Miller in my Jeep and we got there as fast as we could. Then her manager called with the news about the break-in attempt.

Bethany, being Bethany, thanked Asmondius very politely for the care given to her all these years. She was still polite when she asked him why nobody had ever made contact with her to let her know about her heritage and the possibility of it coming to life at an inconvenient time.

"My dear child, your mother didn't want you to know about her side of your heritage, and just when were we to break it to you that you have Fae blood, when we never found reason to contact your father's family for three generations back?" Asmondius said.

"It might have helped," Ben said. "Could I get some of that testing you've been talking to Bethany about? Just in case there is something that should have awakened?"

"Well ... it appears we underestimated you, lad." He nodded. "The events of the last few years have impressed on us that we have grown lax since commerce with the Human realms have been cut back. Harry's cousin, Alexi and his bride are a rather glaring -- no, not a kind word. A shining example ... well, let's just say that they are some of the good results from our looking inward instead of paying attention to the, shall we say, wild oats and hide-bound thinking we have suffered under without even realizing it."

Then his serious expression returned. As serious as a man could be, dressed in a dozen shades of lavender and purple robes, with a purple owl drowsing on his shoulder.

"I'm rather pleased to have discovered that we are distantly related, which will make it somewhat easier for you both to get your testing, and if you wish, the treatment to bring your Fae heritage to the fore. But I hope you remain here in Neighborlee, and in the Human realms, and continue the vital contribution you both make to the duty of guarding this portal between multiple realms, which is your home."

"I thought it was considered a weak spot that needed either

reinforcing or plugging," I couldn't help saying.

"Yes, well ..." Asmondius gave me an admonishing look, but it didn't last long. He winked.

"Just how are we related?" Bethany asked. Her expression was still thoughtful, her gaze distant, and I had the feeling she asked without really being interested. It was just to keep the conversation going while she thought really hard. I had seen that look since she was two years old.

"The easiest description is great-great-grand-cousins. Andreablissa arrived soon after the settling of this town, specifically to keep an eye on the weak spots that were no longer being kept plugged, thanks to tribal warfare wiping out the shamans who were our agents. She was quite happy to settle down here and was the original proprietor of Divine's Emporium before it was an emporium."

"Wait." I had to wrap my mind around the idea. "Angela hasn't been here since there was a Neighborlee?"

"My, do I look that old?" Angela murmured, feigning a distressed look. That got smiles from all of us.

"You look the same as you did the first time I came in here, and you know it," I shot back. She wrinkled up her nose at me. "Sorry. It just ... you're knocking loose a couple dozen foundations right now."

"Yes, well, that's what happens when the children grow up faster than we like." Asmondius nodded. "As I was saying, Blissa built her first cabin on the spot where Divine's now stands. That was necessary. She quickly built quite a successful business providing meals to the quarry workers and the men processing the trees for building lumber, and she passed her incredible culinary skills down to all her descendants. She married Abel Miller and had three sons and two daughters, only one of whom displayed enough magical potential to take up the guardianship after she ... shall we say, retired back to the Fae realms."

"Is she still alive?" Ben asked.

Chapter Five

Asmondius opened his mouth to answer, then paused. "You know, I'm not sure. After several centuries, we tend to lose track of each other, go our separate ways, have different interests. Blissa was quite devoted to Abel, and when he died … well, our family line has a tendency to be once-and-for-all when it comes to finding our heart matches." He nodded and patted Ben's shoulder, when his face flickered once in that pain over Stephanie's loss that had never healed. "You know what I mean. If you like, I will investigate, see if she's still around, and if she'd like to meet some of her descendants. Maybe you'd both like to take some time off to visit the Realm for a short time. Be aware, though, that the passage of time is never predictable. A few days here could be only a few minutes or a few weeks back home. A month or two there could end up being several years here. It's the currents in the chaos between different realms and dimensions. They swirl forward and backward so unpredictably. Keeps life exciting, I think."

"When it doesn't throw a wrench into things, just at the wrong time," Maurice said. "You know, we have an emergency here, and we send up a distress signal, but by the time you get it, so much time passes here that it doesn't do any good for you to rush to help." He shrugged, which did odd things to his wings. "Just saying."

"Yes, and you are justified." Asmondius's eyes narrowed as he studied Maurice for a few moments. Then he shrugged. "Be that as it may … just be aware that your lives back here could be seriously disrupted if you come to visit all your distant relatives."

"I have people I can trust with the diner for a few weeks or months," Ben said. "You don't have that flexibility, though, hon." He rested a hand on Bethany's shoulder.

"You know, Dad … I don't much care about Hollywood. Maybe this is a good time to cut loose and wave goodbye, while my agent is so iffy and things are weird with the studio." She turned to Harry, who looked a little startled, a little relieved, and was starting to glow. Literally, glow, with a yellowish-green haze and little sparkles radiating from his hair and his ear points. "I've got more important things to think about." She chuckled. "Besides, I'm Athena's maid of honor. I'm not going to go back to the West Coast and letting her plan her wedding without me."

"Too soon to make it a double wedding?" Harry blurted. Then he blushed, in a shifting rainbow of pinks and purples.

"Remember what I said about once-and-for-all," Asmondius said, when the rest of us just stared for a few seconds, and Bethany seemed about to choke. She didn't turn different colors, but I noticed her ears looked even pointier than before, and seemed almost neon, compared to the rest of her face.

Honestly? I was relieved for her. The wackos had come out of the woodwork after Bethany's third movie. She just wasn't made to handle that kind of obsessive weirdness. The sudden wimpiness of her agent, rolling over and doing nothing to protect her career just made the decision to toss it that much easier. It was bad enough she had fans rabid enough to know where she lived and keep watch on her apartment. We all had heard too many horror stories about obsessive fans who imagined relationships with celebrities, to the point that they exploded in fury when they felt promises had been broken and their "beloved" had betrayed them in some way. Even if they had never had any communication, other than rambling fan letters printed in crayon. I did not want that for Bethany, and I was relieved for Ben that he didn't have to have that talk with her.

It was time to come home. Or in her case, stay home. If the studio was going to get touchy because of something someone else did, she didn't really owe them any loyalty. Nothing in her contract bound her to a specific number of guest appearances each year. Nor did it require the studio to have her appear, either. How hard would it be for someone to get a phone call in an episode and announce that her character had vanished in a plane crash or had had an accident and needed drastic surgery, and then have a replacement actress take over? Not hard at all, from what I had seen over the years with different long-running TV shows, when the actor who played a character in season one wasn't available in season three.

Can I say I was glad to have Bethany back home in Neighborlee for the foreseeable future? Her dad was relieved, and so was Harry, who had been willing but not exactly eager to settle in California to look after her. The guy had the soul of a small-town homebody, and he loved Neighborlee almost as much as he loved Bethany.

Ben, Bethany, and Harry left a short time later, and Maurice brought up a question while we were cleaning up.

"So Harry's invisibility problem. How reliable is it?" he asked, fluttering across the table to settle in front of Asmondius. There wasn't much he could do to help clear the table of the dirty dishes and cups and empty teapots, other than use wing power to blow crumbs into a pile for disposal.

I paused with a lapful of plates I was ferrying to the kitchen. Angela paused in the doorway with a teapot in either hand.

"I find the juxtaposition of those two concepts interesting. A problem that is reliable?" Asmondius slowly shook his head. "If you mean, how steady would the invisibility be in helping to defend Bethany, if she should come under attack by the imposter ... Harry has developed more control since he met and bonded with her, but ... no, I'm sorry, I am not the right person to ask. I'm relieved for both their sakes, that he doesn't have to rely on what has been a curse all his life, to defend her. It is very easy for me to imagine these doppelgangers revealing they've been only playing games up until now, and pulling out the big guns, so to speak, when they actually have Bethany in their reach. Better for her to stay here, safe within the reinforced shields of Neighborlee, where her bloodline has set down roots."

"You didn't happen to have anything to do with frightening her sufficiently to abandon her no longer satisfying career, did you?" Angela asked. She would have crossed her arms, but those teapots were still in her hands.

"Such as?" Asmondius' innocent look didn't fool me, or her, for a moment.

I suddenly knew, and I had to laugh, despite being so tired. "Those conveniently placed rabid fans," I said, and pointed at him. "Watching her apartment day and night, waiting for her to come back. If you've had people watching out for her all her life, then you know how she feels about the ones who keep breaking her privacy. Perfect opportunity to make her think it was her own decision."

"It *was* her decision." He held onto his innocent look for a few more moments, then he just looked tired as he nodded and smiled faintly. "In many ways, she reminds me of Blissa when she was very young. When we all were very young. I want to protect her for my cousin's sake, but I want her to choose the path she takes."

"So ..." Maurice looked up from sweeping crumbs into a pile for disposal. "Has anybody else gotten the creepies, wondering why these doppelganger dudes are striking here and on the West Coast, and why they're going after Lanie and Bethany and Dawn and Stanzer? And are they working with the ghoulies hiding in that house in Darbyville, or do we have attacks on two fronts?"

"We?" Asmondius smiled, shaking his head slowly.

"Hey, this is home." He shrugged and I thought his blush gave off a faint haze. It was hard to tell from five feet away, and his head so small to begin with.

"You've come a long way, lad. You always had a strong aversion to injustice, but it needed refining and gaining some perspective."

"And mercy, Holly says."

"That too," Angela said, coming back from the kitchen to join us. "Yes, we need to determine what all three of the targets have in common." She sighed. "And prepare for someone else to become the focus of a new attack, when the enemy realizes they are not succeeding."

"Whatever their goals are," I said. "That's the important part, right? Figure out what they want?"

"What do you four have in common?" Asmondius said. "Perhaps that is what triggered the attacks."

"But Bethany hasn't spent much time with Dawn, and none with Stanzer," Angela mused. "She's only been home for a few weeks, and with the holiday busyness ... " Her gaze went distant and lines I didn't like to see formed around her mouth. "Dawn has more in common with Athena than with Bethany, and more in common with Pete and Meggie than Athena."

"If Dawn is tied into the doppelganger problem," I had to say. "It could be Stanzer. Remember that reaction they got when they went to the Darbyville border and the Hounds got uber-protective."

"Hey, kiddo, we don't need trouble on two fronts," Maurice admonished.

It struck me as ridiculous for him to call me "kiddo," even though I knew he was more than two centuries old. How could I see him as older than me, when he looked like a toy half the time?

~~~~~

Friday, the doppelganger struck again. Outside of Neighborlee. Because it couldn't get through the shield and over the border? London and Sherwood had registered regular attempts by something trying to get through the shield. Each time that alien energy flattened itself against our defenses, they gathered another tiny fragment of data. Hopefully they could put together a whole picture of what we were facing. The problem was that the bits of data were so small, it would take a lot of attempts to build a big enough picture to do us any good. Did we have that much time? It was like trying to rebuild a 5,000-piece jigsaw puzzle that had been put through a landscaping mulcher.

The doppelganger had given up on looking like Daniel. Or Bethany, if it was the same enemy or group of enemies.

This time it walked into the offices of Sheridan Communications, on Rockside Road in Independence ... wearing a Lanie Zephyr suit.

Emphasis on walked. More proof these doppelganger creeps were sloppy and didn't do their homework. Just like the fake Bethany made mistakes, so she was outed quickly enough, this imposter didn't have the details down pat on me, either.

Enough people who worked for Sheridan knew me by then, they freaked out and stared a little. Or maybe it was the near-mini skirt the doppelganger was wearing. In January? Be serious! I saw security photos, and out of the handful of frames that weren't blurred by some kind of weird energy, I have to admit I looked good in that skirt, even though, first, I rarely wore skirts, and second, I would never wear anything above my knees, considering how high it would ride when I was sitting down.

Yeah, like we should be complaining that our enemies were sloppy and oblivious? They certainly made our job easier with all their mistakes.

The question was if we could learn fast enough from their mistakes to win this war.

Daniel's assistant, Francesca, earned a raise that day. While other people in the office were picking their jaws up off the floor from the shock of seeing me, allegedly, on my feet, she put herself in the doppelganger's path, before it could start down the central aisle through the big main room of the office. I saw all this on video
~~~~~

replay from the security system, and she was awesome. Francesca didn't see the blurring of the doppelganger's image that the camera lens picked up. Arthur Sheridan speculated on some mental hocus pocus going on. Maybe the doppelganger and its cohorts didn't even know or suspect security cameras and all sorts of electronic surveillance were focused on them when they tried their tricks. They certainly didn't know enough to overcome those giveaways.

Francesca asked the look-alike what she wanted.

"Hi, my name is Lanie Zephyr, and I really need to talk with your boss, Mr. Sheridan. It's urgent."

More warning signs: I would have spent a couple minutes catching up with Francesca, because we had gotten to know each other over the last few years. She came to a handful of my comedy gigs, and I was in charge of keeping Daniel busy while the office assembled a bash for his last birthday. Her son was interested in going to WBC, and I had promised to bring some information on the theater department and the journalism program the next time I came into the office. Francesca would have known I wouldn't forget what I promised. Plus, there was the fact I was standing, and wearing a skirt. And she knew I wouldn't say "your boss" or "Mr. Sheridan" and most definitely I would not say "urgent." If I urgently needed to talk with Daniel, I would have called him on his cell phone, because he always answered that when he ignored his office phone. Like me, he had special ring tones assigned to different levels of callers: one ring tone for family, one ring tone for friends, and a general ring tone for anyone he didn't know, which meant he always let those calls go to voicemail.

Francesca knew all that.

Even more clear warning signs? It was Friday, with a lot of work to do for Tuesday's edition if the staff of the *Tattler* didn't want to work on Saturday and Sunday. I wouldn't have left the newspaper office in the middle of the day to drive to Independence. I certainly wouldn't show up without Daniel knowing I was coming. If there was something urgent enough to handle face-to-face, requiring me to drive half an hour to Independence, Daniel would have told Francesca I was coming, and to send me through as soon as I arrived, even if he was on the phone.

So Francesca knew no matter how realistic this person was, she wasn't Lanie Zephyr.

"If you want to have a seat, ma'am," she said, and gestured at the waiting room, "I'll see if Mr. Sheridan is available."

The lookalike sat down in the waiting area. Francesca went to her desk and played with her computer until she linked several security cameras from different angles to Daniel's computer. Then she called to tell him there was something of vital importance in an email he needed to see. All this while writing that email, listing her suspicions.

Daniel told me later he should know better than to drink anything, whether hot or cold, while looking at something Francesca sent him when she was in super-spy mode, being careful not to address him by name.

Meanwhile, the people in the office closest to the front and the waiting area were either staring at the lookalike or had decided there was nothing interesting going on and had gone back to their work. Big mistakes for both groups. Staring made the fake me nervous, and the ones who ignored it missed when things got really interesting, really fast.

Daniel caught on to the near-mini skirt and the fact the lookalike was sitting in a regular chair, not a wheelchair. That was all he needed to see to know there was a problem in his office. Especially since he hadn't forgotten about the fake Daniels who approached me twice on New Year's Eve. He called my cell phone and stepped to the door of his office to watch the lookalike.

No reaction, because no sound of the phone ringing in her purse.

My phone ringing would have been embarrassing if I really had been sitting in the office when Daniel called. I had been in a snarky mood a couple weeks ago, and changed the ring tone I had assigned to both his office number and his personal phone number. Specifically, I had changed it from a Gollum sound-alike saying, "Our boss is calling. We is afraid of him, yes, Precious, we is," to the really old novelty song from the 70s, "They're Coming to Take Me Away." (ho ho, he he, ha ha)

But fortunately, I and my phone weren't there in the office. The lookalike didn't react, her phone didn't ring, and she certainly didn't sense Daniel watching her. He stepped back into the office to protect our conversation as soon as I picked up my phone. At that moment, Conrad was sitting on the side of my desk, muffling laughter with his hand pressed over his mouth, because of course he heard the ring tone and he was close enough to see Daniel's name and a caricature of him on the screen.

As soon as Daniel told me what was up, I promised to send help, and told him to stall whatever or whoever it was as long as possible. I didn't even care that Conrad overheard me when I called Kurt, although I did feel a little guilty interrupting his afternoon with Jane. Fortunately, they were planning on hitting Quaker Steak and then a movie at Cinemark Valleyview, and I knew when the movie was starting. They had twenty minutes, so I just hoped they hadn't bought their tickets yet.

"My evil twin is sitting in the reception area of Daniel's office. Want to go corner her and find out what's up?" That was all I said, all Kurt needed to hear. He could figure it out. I wouldn't have called him if I didn't know he was going to be right there with Jane, two miles down the street from the Sheridan office.

We had dreamed up some contingency measures, the next time a doppelganger showed up, and the most important one was for Jane to sneak up on it with the Ghost field. With Kurt and Jane together, the doppelganger wearing my face -- but certainly not my body -- was in for a nasty surprise. If they could capture it using the Ghost field, all the better.

"What's going on?" Conrad asked, once Kurt responded they were flying over, literally, and he'd call back when they had something to report.

"Someone is running around pretending to be me, but they don't know enough about me to get a wheelchair."

He just shook his head, with that "now I've heard everything" expression that, unfortunately, he wore quite often, because yeah, he lived and worked in Neighborlee. I could just imagine the conversation he and Clarice, my former college roommate, would have when he got home for dinner that night.

"The really irritating part is that I've been managing to get up on my own feet a little more often lately, so this skanky chick is messing things up for me when I finally get back on my feet full time."

"Wait." He shook his head again, this time like he was shaking something out that was interfering with his hearing. "Get back on your feet?" He looked down at my wheelchair.

"You know, don't you, that I'm not paralyzed? That I do have feeling in my legs? I just use the wheelchair because my legs go numb at the worst possible times, and my knees fold on me, and it's just safer for everyone if I stay seated. Right?" I caught hold of the front of my desk and pushed with my arms as well as my legs, which were shaking a little bit, mostly from tension. I nudged my wheelchair back with a tiny mind-shove and stood up.

Conrad frowned a little and looked me over, head to foot, like he had never seen me standing up before. Which made no sense, because I had gone to any number of social occasions over the years when I had used canes or crutches, depending on how dressy the occasion was. He had seen me walk.

"Basically, I'm one for the textbooks. Maybe it's not total nerve regeneration, but something has been slowly reworking the connections in my body. That's the layman's version, anyway." I waited until something cleared in his eyes and he nodded. Just to be nasty, and kind of foolish, considering how wobbly my legs felt, I took a few steps away from my desk. "I keep my walking to just at home, when I know I can grab onto something if my legs start going out on me."

Yeah, and catch myself with my telekinesis, and yank my chair over to where I needed it, without risk of freaking out anyone.

"The numbness and weakness are receding, and the spells are smaller and less frequent," I added. "For heaven's sake, Connie, you've seen me at the gym, doing leg crunches, you know my legs work."

"Yeah, but not work, work. You know?"

"I know." I clutched at the desk, keeping myself upright when my left knee folded without much warning.

Conrad hurried to grab my wheelchair, which had rolled away a few more inches than I had intended. Blame the uneven floors in the office. Doggone it, but he looked a little relieved that my legs weren't working all that great.

"So anyway ... this chick running around pretending to be me is really messing things up for me, against the day when I finally get rid of my wheels. People are going to start thinking I'm a liar and a fake."

"Nope," he murmured, "just a lazy wimp pretending to be a gimp."

"Hey, copyright infringement," I said, and reached to slap at him as we both laughed. He had misquoted one of my comedy lines from a few years ago. I should have been flattered that he remembered it.

"So, what does this lookalike want? Revenge?"

"When we catch her, we can ask." I shuddered, wondering if it could be that simple. What did it want? The doppelganger or doppelgangers certainly hadn't made the effort to know us well enough to make the impersonations believable. At least, not for people who really knew us.

And why was it taking so long for Kurt to report on what they found?

Conrad thought for a few moments, then he pulled his shoulders back and got up off the edge of my desk. "I'm going to spread the word to the team, so if this imposter shows up around town, they can do some damage control. And I'm telling you as your boss, not your friend."

For about two seconds I considered arguing with him. Then I realized I just felt too tired, so I nodded and thanked him.

Besides, I needed to get him away from my desk so I could take Kurt's call when he reported in, and not have to worry about what I said. I tried not to smile or look too obviously relieved when Conrad finished the business that had brought him over to my desk in the first place and headed back to his office. Then I had second thoughts, about anybody else in the office listening in. Not from curiosity but because they were my friends as well as my co-workers. I decided I didn't really want to be there while Conrad walked from one section of the building to another and gathered people around. I didn't want to feel people turning to look at me, or in the direction of my desk, while he was letting them know that somebody was picking on Lanie. My co-workers all knew I could take care of myself and had seen me flatten a few people who burst into the office, loaded for bear during elections. Still, they had a very obvious problem seeing past my wheelchair. As soon as they heard about the lookalike creating trouble for me, they would be on the defensive for the poor little crippled girl. It didn't matter that I beat most of them in arm wrestling, I was still a victim of Tiny Tim Syndrome.

So I grabbed my coat and gloves and backpack, and wheeled

down the ramp to the main door. I let Matilda know I was heading out to the Sipping Post. Did she want anything? Of course, she would always want one of the decadent creamy drinks that only bore a faint resemblance to coffee. I had learned long ago to take good care of the receptionist, because she would take good care of me when lunatics came through the door, raving because I didn't feature their darling high school or college athlete. It didn't matter that they didn't live in Neighborlee, their child deserved to be listed in every paper covering the latest basketball game or track meet or whatever sporting event had just happened.

We never had this problem until a water park in the next county started taking pictures of every kid who went down the highest slide and promised their picture would be in the local paper. Then they would send the kids' pictures to us with just their names, not the cities they lived in. Policy was to only feature residents of Neighborlee. We weren't going to waste time looking up every family with that last name and ask if they had a child who had just gone to the waterpark. That kind of phone call in this day and age was more likely to get us visited by the police and child protective services, rather than generate good PR.

Ever since then, sports parents got it into their heads that just seeing a camera pointed in their student athlete's direction was a promise, sealed in blood, that their child's picture would be in the newspaper. I always wondered why, when their child didn't even place, or didn't score any points, or fell flat ten feet from the finish line, or other mistakes and bloopers.

So, out into the sunny, frigid weather I went. I had to remind myself this was only the first full week of January, even if it did feel like we had put in a month's worth of worrying and working and conferencing. I got as far as crossing the street and getting the Sipping Post within view, at the end of the block, when I realized I had made a serious miscalculation.

Just like I couldn't sit in the newspaper office and talk openly with Kurt or Jane about this confrontation with my evil twin, I couldn't do it in the Sipping Post, either. There were bound to be a handful of retirees sitting by the electric fireplace in the corner, and people with books or tablets or newspapers, relaxing in the deep lounge chairs, plus people having late lunches. The acoustics in the Sipping Post discouraged private conversations. I paused to consider my options. The wind picked up, slicing icy air into my face. It wasn't snowing, fortunately but I needed to be somewhere indoors when the call came.

Well, duh -- Stanzer's office. He needed to be included in the latest development, if whatever had riled the Hounds the other day was in league with the doppelgangers. As I rolled along, my brain went in a new direction. I wondered if there was something the Hounds could do if someone wasn't directly threatening him and Dawn. My impression was that they played by their own rules. Stanzer had assured me the Hounds liked me, and that was good, because common sense said not to get on their bad side. The problem was, being liked wasn't the same as being friendly enough to ask for favors. Such as walking patrol and looking out for other interdimensional invaders or visitors or whatever might be trying to break through Neighborlee's defenses.

I looked around for anyone who might be watching. All clear. Everyone seemed to be indoors, busy with errands. Hopefully nobody would be watching long enough to notice a wheelchair zipping down the cleared sidewalks faster than walking speed. And with no arm movements to keep the wheels turning. I hunkered down a little for less wind resistance, hid my face deeper in my scarf, took a deep breath, and gave a hard mental shove to my wheels. At times like these, I was grateful my broken back had only taken away my kinda-sorta flying ability, and not my telekinesis. Pretty handy in icy weather like this.

The crosswalk light was green when I got to the final intersection before Stanzer's building. I still saw nobody close enough to notice what I was doing, so I gave another hard shove and zipped across the intersection even faster than I had been before. Kind of like the way I drove in the middle lane when I crossed that suicidally high I-480 bridge at Valleyview. This intersection always gave me a shudder. Jay Parker had tried to run me down here with his truck, two Christmases ago, when he and Toby Malone and Steve Muldoon had been programmed by the Rivals to hunt me.

Chapter Six

I got to the other side and made a sharp right turn on the corner, to head for the door of Stanzer's PI office. At the other end of the block, I saw Dawn trudging up the street. That threw me for a moment, until I let go control of the wheels, let my chair slow down, and checked my watch. 2:45pm. The senior high would be letting out soon. If Dawn had a study hall for final period, as a senior she had the option of getting out early. She was smart, she was always ahead of her class assignments, it only made sense for her to get out as soon as she could. I waved to her and paused as I reached the office door. Her head came up and she picked up her pace, and I was relieved to see her smiling. Dawn was way too somber most of the time.

Movement from the corner of my eye had me turning, to see Stanzer standing in the big picture window of his office, watching her come. Something squeezed at my heart, seeing the aching and hopelessness and what had to be a spark of frustration in his expression. No matter how rough it had to be for Dawn, twelve years instead of four years younger than the man who had once been her best friend in their home world, it had to be twice as bad for Stanzer. His main focus all the years he had been alone was finding Dawn, his betrothed, and joining forces to find the rest of the Hunt. Now he had found her, but she was still legally a minor.

Sometimes I wanted to yank the Hounds around by the scruff of their necks, whack their backsides with a newspaper, and yell, "Bad dog, bad dog, look at the mess you made," a dozen times. Only someone with a death wish would try that.

"Hey, what's up?" I called to Dawn, to stop myself thinking in that direction before a Hound overheard me. There was no telling when one of them would show up.

"Thank God for the weekend!" she called back and scurried the last dozen sidewalk squares. "Are you joining us for movie night?"

"Ah … sounds like fun, but I'm here mostly looking for shelter and maybe a sympathetic ear that won't get freaked out."

"Uh huh. You came to the right place." She stepped around me and reached for the doorknob.

Stanzer got there first, pushed it open, and stepped outside to hold the door for me until I slid up the ramp and into his office. She chattered for a few moments as we took off our coats and he moved a few chairs around so I could park my wheelchair by his desk. Most of it was the titles she had selected for their Friday night of movies, picked up at the library, and the order she had placed for pizza and wings to be delivered.

It sure sounded like date night to me. Even if I had been free that evening, I wouldn't have intruded.

When we were settled, I explained about my evil twin at the Sheridan office, and needing a place indoors where I could take the report and talk without freaking out anyone who might overhear my side of the conversation. Stanzer was just starting to ask me questions about how this tied into the New Year's Eve encounter when my phone rang. It was the main theme for Beauty and the Beast -- my ringtone for Jane. Kurt hadn't heard it yet, and I was still living in anticipation of his reaction when he realized the joke and implications.

"I swear," Jane said, as soon as I said hello, "we're dealing with some freaky new breed of vampires."

"Vampires?"

That got a cocked eyebrow from Stanzer, and Dawn choked on the big mouthful of hot chocolate she had just taken.

"Apparently daylight turns them to dust."

"Then how did that thing get into Daniel's office in the first place? And aren't they supposed to burst into flames in daylight?"

Yeah, that last was totally stupid to say. Since when did the vampires in *Buffy the Vampire Slayer* have anything to do with real-life nasty creatures of the soul-and-blood-sucking variety? If they existed in reality.

"Wait," I hurried to say before Jane could answer. "I'm at Stanzer's. Let me put you on speaker. Is Kurt there?"

I tapped the control for speaker and set my phone on the desk, where it could pick up all our voices.

"He's downstairs, dealing with the custodian and the landlord and a couple other tenants of the building, who are pretty freaked out. Turns out this building suddenly has a tunnel that isn't part of the original plans. The landlord runs his leasing operation out of this building, and he's the original owner, meaning he built it. You can imagine he's freaked out to find that tunnel." Jane exhaled loudly. "The walls are packed dirt, very even, like something big and strong pressed them flat, but … according to readings we took before all unholy heck broke loose, Kurt thinks it was dug just in the last few days."

"Makes sense," Stanzer said. "What happened?"

"The thing freaked out as soon as we flew in. The one on New Year's didn't sense us in the Ghost field, but this one did. Maybe they learn from experience. Maybe they're sending smarter and more alert ones. The moment we came through the wall, it started screaming and backed away from us and ran for it. Someone was coming up the stairs, otherwise I think it would have knocked the door off its hinges. It hunched down in on itself the closer it got to the light coming through the window at the end of the hall. We got ahead of it, racing down the stairs, and were waiting on the first-floor landing. It swerved and shrieked and went out the landing door, through the lobby. As soon as it stepped outside through the tinted plate glass wall, it kind of went up in smoke, or dust or something. It just vanished."

"So it didn't go down the tunnel?" Dawn said. "How did you find the tunnel?"

"We followed the energy trail it left when it came in."

"So when the one at New Year's vanished after it got through the shield, it didn't just disappear, it disintegrated?" I said, testing the theory by speaking it. "Okay, I'm officially creeped out."

"You're not the only one," Jane said. "Six people saw that thing come racing outside and just go *poof*. Fortunately, it didn't look anything like you by the time it got down the stairs."

"Oh, that's a relief."

"Hey, I'm in Daniel's office, so we can get some privacy, but they're going to come for me for a statement soon. We didn't become visible until the thing ran from us in the lobby, so we're just witnesses, but the guys she knocked over at the top of the stairs know what floor she came from, and Daniel's office takes up the entire floor. They've already tracked things back to him. I need to get together with Kurt and Daniel and figure out what official story to give the cops and whoever else shows up. I just wanted to let you know, since we figured you're waiting."

"Yeah, thanks."

When Jane hung up, Stanzer, Dawn and I just sat there for a few minutes, looking at each other.

"That just isn't right," he said, breaking the silence. "Freaky stuff like that isn't supposed to happen outside Neighborlee."

I thought about the man who tried to steal my Jeep early in the summer, one of Kerri's minions. That had happened outside our town limits, so it was another strike against what we considered the rules or the norm. But I could understand what Stanzer meant.

"That's the worst part," I said, thinking aloud again. I really had to stop doing that, but right that moment my brain was working way too slowly. "The shield around Neighborlee is getting stronger, so we should be safer. Either the weird stuff is leaking out some weak spot London hasn't found, or the weird stuff that would normally come inside can't get inside, so it's happening outside."

Later I realized another problem. The protective amnesia that helped residents of Neighborlee live with the weirdness, by making them either ignore it when it happened under their noses, or forget it as soon as it happened, wasn't outside. All those witnesses to the lookalike going nuts and then turning to dust didn't have that nice Neighborlee mental defense. What were our chances that someone would investigate until the weirdness trail led them to us? When the investigators stepped inside the boundaries of our town, would the Neighborlee defensive magic get to work fixing things, maybe rewriting memories, or spectacularly and inconveniently fail us?

~~~~~

Arthur Sheridan asked Mum and Pop to investigate the tunnel the lookalike dug to get to the office building without going into the daylight. We really hoped they weren't vampires of a new variety. There were designs pressed into the dirt walls of the tunnel, and maybe they would provide some answers. Maybe they were part of an old kind of magic, and maybe the designs could be tracked to a source, to give us some answers. The owner of the building was a friend of Arthur, which was the main reason Sheridan Corporation set up their offices there when they expanded into Northeast Ohio. Unfortunately, that friend wasn't a Neighborlee resident, which would have gone a long way toward helping cover over the mess.
~~~~~

Mum and Pop showed up first thing Saturday morning, taking advantage of the low weekend population in the building, and got to work. Their plan was to go to the very end of the tunnel, wherever that ended up being, taking video of all the walls as they went in, using a 360-degree camera Kurt whipped up overnight. Of course, Kurt came with them to operate the camera.

I thank God Kurt was there. Mum and Pop got twenty feet or so inside the tunnel, then that telltale humming in the air and tingling in his fingers revealed some kind of energy at work. It got stronger with every step the three of them took into the tunnel. To be specific, five steps. Kurt listened to the instincts we all had honed after years of dealing with weirdness.

He got my folks out of there, and we were all grateful. The tunnel didn't so much collapse as the compressed dirt of the walls un-compressed and went back where it belonged.

Meaning my folks and Kurt would have been squashed, or at least quickly suffocated.

Harry (Bethany's Harry, to be clear), Kurt, and Jane went back to the office building that night, after everything had shut down, to investigate. The really frightening part of all this? There were only faint traces of some kind of power in the dirt where there used to be a tunnel. It faded fast as Jane studied it with the Ghost field. Then Harry examined it using some Fae techno gear that Kurt said gave him hives when he tried to touch it. I could imagine how his mouth was watering at the thought of examining something made by Fae, with magic woven into whatever mechanical wizardry was going on. However, the energy resonance clashed with whatever made us semi-pseudo-superheroes.

Harry didn't get much from the fading magical energy residue. At least, he thought it was magic, but it didn't feel like the Fae magic he understood. It was too strange, half a step out of phase with what he had dealt with all his life. Fae magic, but not Fae magic. It reminded him of nursery tales his nanny and grandmother used to tell him, about rebel Fae who had caused enough trouble to get themselves exiled to a sideways dimension. Chances were, most modern Fae didn't believe in those stories, if they thought of them at all. Which meant finding someone who could identify the energy, the resonance, and know how to respond and deal with it, could be tricky.

This was all way out of his reach, his area of expertise. He was going to have to go back to the Fae Realms and dig up -- hopefully, not literally -- some of the more ancient researchers who spent years investigating far distant realms and rumors of warping magic. He got copies of the images Mum and Pop recorded before the tunnel started decompressing, in case they could be clues.

Jane sent a report of her impressions to Hoax, on the chance one of their insane geniuses might have a gizmo or some theories that would be useful here. Kurt and Jane spent some time in conference with London and Sherwood, tracking down the readings they had gotten from the New Year's Eve doppelganger's entrance and attempts to exit through the shield. Maybe they could get something there to send to Hoax to work on.

Our friendly AI's had been focusing on expanding their sensitivity so they could detect the out-of-phase vibrations of the doppelganger and his friends. Besides being able to detect when this new nemesis approached the Neighborlee shield, Sherwood hoped to come up with detectors we could wear, to warn us if danger approached whenever we were outside the borders of our town.

I wondered how long it would take until the goldfish bowl syndrome settled in, when we all felt like none of us were safe to leave our town.

My mind kept snagging on that little bit Harry had told us before he left, about it being Fae magic, but not Fae magic. Like maybe it had started out as Fae magic, but got warped? If there was anything formerly Fae about it, what did that tell us about this enemy facing us? Had the doppelgangers and their bosses or allies once been Fae, but turned to the Dark Side?

Of course, that thinking led me to a meme I had seen a few months before, proclaiming that when Elves went bad, they went Marvel bad. The images were of a number of actors as their characters in the *Lord of the Rings* and *Hobbit* movies, and then as Marvel villains. When I first saw it, I thought it was clever and wryly funny. I wasn't smiling anymore, and it kind of gave me chills.

~~~~~

On Monday, Bethany called her agent. She told him in an email beforehand that she wanted a private conversation about her
~~~~~

career. The obstinate jerk set up a conference call with the studio and Nickelodeon series people without telling her. Bethany started the conversation referencing the last email she had sent her agent, which he hadn't responded to yet. He obviously hadn't read it because he blew up at her after only three sentences. While the studio and Nickelodeon people were listening.

I know, because Bethany had me, Athena, her father, and Angela there to listen. We weren't there to participate, except yeah, Ben would have jumped in if he got a chance. We were there for moral support, emotional support, and to act as witnesses if things got messy. Bethany was worried they would because her agent hadn't responded to any of her concerns.

While her agent, the studio and Nickelodeon people took turns scolding Bethany and expressing a bare minimum of sympathy for all the trouble she was dealing with, someone was listening in. Not just listening, but recording and streaming it, live, on the Internet. Sherwood was monitoring the phone call to help us, in case there was some sabotage -- and there was. He sent messages to all our phones and tablets. Athena pulled out her computer and got to work, trying to track down things. Sherwood went after the perpetrator while Athena went after the social media sabotage. It wasn't pretty, and that was putting it mildly.

The studio rep threatened to sue her for breach of implied promises, because of screen tests Bethany had missed, which she had never heard about. Her agent denied that the screen tests had been agreed to. Bethany asked what movie they were talking about. That turned into a he-said-she-said round of denials and accusations about a script her agent never mentioned to her. The studio guy said he had sent it. The agent claimed he never received it. The Nickelodeon rep kept trying to break in and calm things down. How many times can someone try to be heard over an increasingly nasty back-and-forth, on the phone, before they become a target and turn from trying to make peace to avoiding being verbally flayed? Before the Nickelodeon rep hung up, Bethany's character on the show had been condemned to die an embarrassing and permanent death.

Well, that was some relief. Until the fallout from all the accusations and claims and counterclaims and threats of lawsuits on both sides spread across social media. The studio and the agent accused each other until they made Bethany the scapegoat.

The uproar from Bethany's fans, outrage over how she had been treated, was gratifying for a short while. People played clips from the phone conversation to defend her as an abused victim of power-hungry, egotistical jerks.

That defense didn't last long. Within a day, people got hold of the recording of that disastrous conference call and edited it so Bethany came across as either a stoned little twit or a prima donna with Machiavellian tendencies. Depending on who did the editing and what their goals were.

Her agent responded with a public announcement that he was releasing Bethany from her contract. He was quoted by unidentified sources as saying he was relieved to be free of her, she had been trouble for months, and she would be doing the world a favor by vanishing permanently.

This from the guy who had alternated between pleading and a strong-arm routine to keep her from taking more than two days off for Christmas. He had offers for her to do guest appearances nearly every day between Christmas and Valentine's Day.

Now suddenly she was anathema? Something was up.

We really had to wonder if that was more nastiness from the same people who sent the doppelganger. What did they want with Bethany? Was someone operating some really nasty, nuclear war magic on her, and if so, why? What did the enemy want? Why go after Bethany?

Maybe she really would be better off if she took Asmondius' offer, had the Fae equivalent of gene therapy, and headed for the Fae Realms for a few years?

Before that depressing thought could settle in, we got more questions and a few answers. The problem was, sometimes having answers wasn't exactly a good thing.

Simon Jones, a private investigator, tapped three times on the glass of Stanzer's front door on Thursday and walked into his office. Seriously? Who knocks on the door of a business before entering?

The guy wore a black suit. Not the shabby Blues Brothers style of black suit. Rather stylish, actually, but the all-black ensemble got our attention. It was a blustery kind of day, and the guy didn't have a hat or gloves, and he didn't button his outer coat. Black, stylish, and visibly paired with the suit underneath it. One point in his favor: he wasn't wearing sunglasses, on a day that was so overcast a flashlight might have been helpful at 2 in the afternoon.

I know, because I was visiting Stanzer, discussing his concern for Dawn, and coming up with some contingency plans for when he needed to leave town for more than three hours at a time. It was the nature of the business that Stanzer might have to do overnight trips for investigations. Angela had suggested that if Dawn was a target, the enemy might take the tactic of getting Stanzer out of town to take away her most alert defender, then send someone to snatch her on her way home from school. We were discussing the communication system and the relay of watchers and even couriers, if necessary, so Dawn would never be alone. Her most vulnerable time would be on the trip from school to Divine's Emporium, mostly because she would have to cross Overlook Avenue. It was the main drag through town, used to get from one highway entrance ramp to another, and to business and industrial parks. It was all fine and good to know the Hounds would pop into our dimension of reality at a moment's notice, but they weren't that reliable. Dawn needed to be *aware* she was in trouble to summon the Hounds, if the enemy wasn't focusing so intently on her that they set off alarms that the Hounds caught while waiting in another dimension. We were debating getting her a car to drive, or having guardians take turns picking her up and driving her, when the knock came on the door.

"Hey, sorry," Jones said, rocking back on his heels when he saw me sitting opposite Stanzer in my wheelchair. "I can come back when you're not busy with a client." He flashed a thin smile. "Professional courtesy."

"Not a client," I said. I had an urge to grab hold of the guy's hand and pray for a vision, for my unreliable telepathic foresight to kick in and tell me what the guy was thinking and planning. I did not trust anyone who walked around in the rotten weather we had that day without a hat or gloves.

Then a second later, I realized he was Men in Black stylish. Maybe a little too stylish for a private investigator, starting with that snazzy embossed identification wallet he snapped open to show Stanzer his investigator's license and ID photo. Some people might have felt a well-dressed private investigator guaranteed a successful job done for them, but my cynical side saw those fancy threads as just a warning the guy overcharged for his services.

I pulled my wheelchair back and gestured for him to step up to Stanzer's desk, which he did, introducing himself and visibly dismissing me. Wrong move. Never turn your back on a cranky semi-pseudo-superhero in a wheelchair. We have a tendency to accidentally-on-purpose ram your ankles with our foot pedals. And that's just for starters.

I pushed aside my irritation as Jones explained why he needed Stanzer's help. Which should have been a warning sign, not professional courtesy, as he kept calling it.

I had to wonder just how professional this guy was, because he did not do his homework before stepping into Stanzer's office. Then again, his clients may have been messing him over from the beginning. Lying to him. *Alleged* clients. We had no proof there really were clients as opposed to an evil overlord, making him a minion instead of a hired investigator.

All this guy had to work from were photos, which he slapped down on Stanzer's desk like they were exhibits in a trial. We learned later that before he came into Stanzer's office, he drove around town for an hour or two in his black sedan, catching too much attention by driving ten miles under the speed limit and stopping frequently to snap pictures. People, buildings, scenery, road signs. He never talked to anyone, never asked questions, never tried to get information. What private investigator doesn't talk to anyone except the local PI?

Especially when the person he was investigating was the under-age girl under Stanzer's guardianship.

Chapter Seven

Yep, he had big eight-by-ten photos of Dawn, taken from long distance. There were other people in the photos, starting with me. Yet this hotshot PI looked me in the face and didn't recognize me. Granted, in the photos I was standing up, leaning against my Jeep, talking to Dawn. Only the top couple inches of my wheelchair were visible in the photo. Someone who didn't know I had a wheelchair wouldn't have realized what it was. Still, the guy should have studied the photos long enough to recognize me when he looked me in the face.

Just goes to prove that there's a kind of cloaking field when it comes to wheelchairs. People look right at us, but they don't actually *see* us. Just our chairs. Or whatever other visible physical handicap we have.

Stanzer gave me a sideways look and adjusted one of the photos, enough I could get a better angle. Mister Oblivious Hotshot PI never noticed. Never even glanced at me, wondering why Stanzer was letting me see the photos. He was too busy with his spiel, talking about how his client was looking for a missing granddaughter, whom they believed had taken shelter in our town. A troubled girl. A runaway. A consummate liar. And yet despite the pain she had caused her loving family, she was treasured and missed, and they were horribly concerned for her welfare. It was a high priority that she not know her family had located her whereabouts. They simply wanted to make sure she was safe, that she had found shelter with good people, and the local authorities could be depended on to support them when they chose to take custody.

Did he know the name this alleged runaway was using? No.

Did he know where she was living? No.

Did he know where the photos had been taken? No.

Did he know when they were taken? No.

Did he know who the people were in the photos? No.

The people alone were a dead giveaway. Other than me, the

other people appearing in the photos with Dawn were students and teachers at Neighborlee High. They were all in the background, not interacting with her. The few objects appearing in the background of the photos were cars and portions of the decorative sandstone facing of Neighborlee High.

One other person appeared in the photos, interacting with Dawn. Bethany Miller. The two of them were sitting on the decorative half-wall in front of the front doors of the high school building, engaged in an apparently involved conversation that went back and forth between laughter and frowns, with lots of hand gestures.

I wheeled up as close as I could get to the desk, and while PI Simon Jones was giving Stanzer the story his alleged clients gave him, and while his head was turned, I used my telekinesis to turn the photos and flip through them, little by little, so I could get a good look at all of them. An image formed in my mind, so by the time Jones handed Stanzer his business card, thanked him for his help, and left, with the promise Stanzer would call if he came up with anything, I had a good theory.

Good because it kind of made sense. *Bad, nasty,* and *dangerous* because of the implications that came with that theory.

"Serenity?" I blurted, once Jones had disappeared from the big picture window at the front of the office, and the sound of the obnoxiously powerful engine in his car faded into the distance. "Who would ever slap a name like that on Dawn?"

Yeah, that was the name Jones's clients claimed for this missing, rebellious granddaughter, who couldn't be told that rescue was on its way for fear she would hit the road once again. I mean, my folks were hippies, but they knew better than to try to hang a name like that on me when they adopted me.

"Doesn't matter, because that isn't her name." Stanzer looked down at his desk, where the pictures had been lying. Jones couldn't leave the photos because he didn't have spares. What decent PI doesn't have duplicates of everything, especially photos? Especially when he's asking for help from other PIs? Even more suspicious, he twitched a few times as Stanzer made copies of them. Like he wanted to protest but was afraid to.

"Those pictures were all taken from one location." I waited for him to raise his head and look at me. "Across the street from the high school. On the property of that old flower shop building where nobody is able to stay in business very long." I wanted to smile when dawning comprehension widened Stanzer's eyes, but all I could do was shiver a little.

From the grim line of Stanzer's mouth, he remembered the whole incident, with Pi Surprise and Kerri and her contract woven with evil magic. It was kind of nice that he remembered, because the whole mess had occurred while he was trying to figure out how to get Dawn out of the protective custody of federal agents.

Did the angle of the camera that caught the photos of Dawn, Bethany and me, on the property of that old flower shop, provide proof that Kerri and her black-suited, pale minions had returned for round two?

"So … if they're standing across the street, taking pictures … does that mean they aren't any more able to come into Neighborlee than the doppelgangers?" Stanzer murmured, after several moments of silence.

"Would explain why they sent that pitiful excuse for a PI, and why he doesn't know she's with you," I said.

"Unless they're all just playing games to get more information. Maybe make us complacent and relax, so we make mistakes. Maybe the big mistake is to believe Dawn is the target, when they're aiming at someone else, and they want us focused on her to distract us." He sighed and finally sat down at his desk. "Can't risk that, though. Not with the way the Hounds reacted last week. All the pictures were taken at the high school? Why were you there?" he added, when I nodded.

"Career day, talking to the kids about journalism. Dawn had some questions about stories she had heard, things going on at Eden and the high school. Weird stuff. She just wanted help figuring out what was real and what was tall tales made to freak out the new kid. We had a good laugh at how many stories were pretty real, and weirder than most people could ever imagine."

"I can imagine." A flicker of humor lit his eyes for a moment. "There was a short time after I got here that I was hearing the stories and wondering just what I had gotten myself into. Even with the Hounds giving their stamp of approval, and Angela giving me a basic orientation speech." The humor fled and he shook his head, frowning in thought. "So we can avoid Dawn getting spied on if she parks in the back lot and doesn't go out the front door. Think we should warn all our gang to avoid the front door, being seen from that building?"

"That's a good idea. Until we figure out what Kerri wants. Gotta wonder what's keeping them from just crossing the street and confronting Dawn while she's out in the open on school property. The shield wasn't that strong back in October when those pictures were taken of me. Why didn't they come through back then?"

"The Hounds, for one thing."

"Wouldn't we know, or at least Dawn would know, if they tried at least once? I bet when we talk to her, she never got a flicker of warning, no sign of the Hounds showing up and reacting to a threat. Not like New Year's."

"True." His frown deepened. "So they aren't trying anything. Does it have to do with timing? What are they preparing for? Maybe they waited too long, and now they can't get through the shield either? With the computer kids playing with the shield, maybe we can keep them out altogether?"

"I like that idea. Especially if they're resorting to using outsiders. The not knowing why worries me. I mean, yeah," I hurried to say, when he opened his mouth to respond. I could pretty much guess what he was going to say. "Yeah, the shield is keeping them out, but ... there has to be more than that energy. Other nasties have come into town without any trouble. What's stopping Kerri?"

"Kerri and her crew are the doppelgangers?"

"Now you're depressing me."

That got a snort and a brief smile from him. "So we know what you were doing there. What was Bethany doing there, and when, that she got her picture taken?"

When we called her to find out, Bethany was busy with the first influx of kids getting out of school and arriving at Millers, and she said she would call us back. That gave us a new concern: How much did we tell Dawn? She would be back from school soon. She had a right to know about this new threat, and it was just plain stupid to keep her in the dark and treat her like a little kid who couldn't participate in defending herself. Stanzer had learned that the hard way last summer, nearly losing Dawn just when he had found her.

While we were waiting for Bethany to call back, I went through what I could remember of that afternoon at the high school. I honestly couldn't say if I sensed something, or I just let the proximity of that decrepit old building and the memories of what had happened last summer bother me, maybe influence my perceptions. I did have some weird sensations, a momentary chill when I was crossing the parking lot to the school. When I came outside again, I was too busy talking with Dawn to notice any otherness or threat. Stanzer was right. If there had been a threat to Dawn, specifically, the Hounds would have reacted. Meaning whoever was watching us and taking pictures was only doing that. They weren't planning an attack or thinking angry or hateful thoughts focused on Dawn.

Bethany called, and she was just starting to answer my questions about why she was at the high school, and when, and if she remembered talking to Dawn in the parking lot, when Dawn came back from school. Stanzer took her aside to talk, in low voices, leaving me to make notes on what Bethany said.

The story was fairly simple. The first day back at school, Monday after New Year's Eve, Bethany went to talk to the drama classes about acting, about her start in community theater and doing commercials. She had run into the drama teacher, Mr. Shelton, at the New Year's party at Eden, and they had had so much fun reminiscing about the theater productions when she was in school, he insisted she had to share her memories. When she was done talking to the students, Dawn caught up with her. She got early dismissal, as a senior, and walked with Bethany out to the parking lot.

What did they talk about? Basically, comparing notes and experiences. What it was like for Dawn, knowing she was from another world, and had essentially forgotten much of it for a few years, for the sake of survival and her sanity. Then, what it was like for Bethany, learning her mixed magical heritage so late in her life. Having grown up in Divine's Emporium with Angela for her godmother, seeing so many odd things all her life, she had considered them normal. Until now, looking back.

"She said you suggested putting together a survivor's club," I added, when I finished my report for Stanzer and Dawn, less than ten minutes after hanging up with Bethany. There wasn't that much to report. She hadn't sensed anything weird at the time, but then, Bethany was still learning to use her magical senses.

"I was joking!" Dawn put up her hands as if blocking a blow, but she was grinning. Stanzer only showed a flicker of confusion, or maybe hurt feelings, before he grinned back at her. Okay, so things were still good between them. "And yeah, I was feeling kind of awkward. I mean, Bethany Miller, you know? Someone I wanted to be like, when I saw her movie last summer. And she was standing there and asking for advice from *me*, on the whole adjusting to an otherworldly heritage problem. Don't you always say something really dumb when you're feeling like you're totally knocked off beat and balance?"

"Unfortunately. Not that I'll ever admit to saying that," I hurried to add. "I'm a grownup. Or at least I'm supposed to be." I stopped myself just in time from adding, "You're a kid, enjoy the awkward time while you can." No sense in reminding her and Stanzer of the big gap of years between them.

He had caught her up on what the PI wanted, and they had been looking at the pictures he had copied, while I was finishing up with Bethany. We settled down at the conference table on the far side of the office and talked about both times in the parking lot at school, trying to find anything Dawn remembered or sensed that Bethany and I hadn't caught.

"Yeah ... about that ..." She turned around her half-empty mug of hot chocolate a few times, clearly avoiding looking at either of us. "The thing is ... I've been avoiding that parking lot out front. It's just felt weird for the last couple months. I mean, I thought it was because of that ultimate bozo, Bidenski. It's like he's staked a claim on that area as his domain, you know?"

"Uh, no," I said. "Who is he?"

"Biggest jerk and bully in the school. He was picking on some freshmen. I mean, these kids were really small for their age. And I ..." She took a deep breath and met our gazes, just for a few seconds each, before studying her hands again. "I kind of got between them and him and made them -- made us -- vanish ... for a few seconds."

"How?" I blurted, when Stanzer just groaned.

"There was a Hound, wasn't there?" he said. Dawn nodded. "That's how Dawn got away from the Feds protecting her last summer. If we're holding onto a Hound, we can go invisible, even walk through walls if we're teamed up. You caught hold of the kids and made them vanish, and Bidenski freaked out?"

"It was great. And nobody realized what happened, because I got the kids running and we were around the corner of the building and they didn't even see the Hound and ..." She sighed. "But he saw me get between him and the other kids. He was making threats about how I had to show him how I pulled the vanishing act, and he could make us both rich and I'd be really sorry if I didn't. So I just thought all the creepy-crawly I feel when I'm in the front parking lot came from him waiting for me." She shrugged. "The only time I've gone in that parking lot is when I'm with someone else."

"You probably sent up a flare of some kind of energy when you called on the Hound for help," Stanzer said with a sigh. "That got the attention of whoever or whatever is hiding in that building across the street, and they've been watching."

"How would they know it's Dawn they want?" I asked.

"She probably left a trail, enough energy residue for them to get her scent or ..." He shrugged. "They're focused on Dandova." He flinched, and it showed just how worried he was that he used her real name, instead of calling her Dawn, which she preferred.

"Okay, so they know me, because I've come up against them before, and they probably know Bethany because her face is all over magazines and movie posters and teen gossip sheets. The first fake Bethany sighting came the day after she had that talk at the school." I paused, waiting for a nebulous idea to solidify.

"They aren't able to track anyone down inside the shield. Maybe the energy that keeps them from crossing over makes them blind? Other than what they can see with their physical eyes. If that makes sense," he added, his voice dying away. He frowned, not liking what he was theorizing aloud. I could understand that, because I didn't like it, and he was pretty much voicing what I was thinking.

Then Dawn shuddered and her face wrinkled up like she was going to be sick, or she had just had an awful thought. Stanzer caught hold of her shoulder.

"What?" he demanded.

"Just before Christmas break ... Bidenski got some kids to trick me into coming to the front parking lot, and then he just came out of nowhere and grabbed my arm and tried to drag me across the street. He wanted to talk to me in private, he said. Coach Sheffield was there and stopped him before I could even think to call the Hound. But what if he was trying to get me into that building? It isn't directly across the street, but close enough."

"Getting you out of Neighborlee and beyond the shield might have been enough," I had to say. I didn't want to. Stanzer let go to wrap his arm around her shoulders.

"This bully works for the enemy now?" he muttered.

"He might not even know he does. He could be a dupe, just like the PI, Jones. At least, I hope Jones is a dupe. He didn't seem upset that there are all sorts of holes in the information they gave him."

We tossed ideas and theories back and forth for a little while, until we agreed we needed to investigate that old building. How could we do that without opening ourselves up to attack, and without them seeing us and finding a new target for their tricks and attacks? In the end, we called Jane and Kurt to help us using the Ghost field. I accompanied them, to describe what happened. If anything happened.

There was definitely something there in the old building, and the Ghost field let us sneak up on it. We hovered on the Neighborlee side of the street long enough to determine that whatever was in the building didn't know we were there. So we decided to get closer.

Kurt and Jane both described it as a dark, oily, churning fog hunkering down close to the ground. If that was the next alien invader itself, or just some camouflage keeping us from seeing what was really there, they couldn't be sure. Looking back, I have to wonder why we wanted to find out for sure. Usually when something nasty goes to some trouble to keep itself hidden from view, that's a pretty good sign we don't want to know. Am I right?

The cloud monster didn't react, didn't give any indication it knew we were there, hopefully invisible inside the Ghost field.

Until Jane, who was doing the driving, moved the bubble of the Ghost field over the border between Neighborlee and Cutterville.

I didn't see the oily dark churning fog they had described to me until we were about halfway across the road between the high school property and the lot with the decrepit flower building. Then it became visible to me. It was too much like that vision we had picked up last summer when Maurice figured out how to look backward in time and read that tricky contract Kerri tried to get me to sign. The cloudy darkness surrounding the building was a lot like what I saw in the pool of water that let us see and eventually hear and physically reach through time to rescue my folks.

That cloudy darkness sort of sat up and came to attention when the Ghost field moved across to the Cutterville side of the road. How a churning mass of fog could do that, when it didn't have a face and it didn't have a head to turn or a body to sit up and come alert, I don't know. That was just the impression I got.

"That thing is not happy," Kurt muttered. "Jane --"

"On it," Jane snapped, and the Ghost field slammed into reverse, throwing us back across the street and over the border into Neighborlee.

The churning black fog followed us. Or more accurately, this long pseudopod of churning darkness reached out from the mass, like the Blob or some nasty anime ooze shooting at us.

As soon as we were safely back inside Neighborlee, I couldn't see the fog anymore. From the mixture of revulsion and amazement on Kurt and Jane's faces, I knew I should be grateful. Whatever they were staring at, as we hovered about thirty feet up in the air over the apron of the driveway into the high school parking lot, it wasn't pretty.

"Uh, what's it doing?" I finally asked, when they both had flinched a few times.

"It's ... " Jane shrugged and looked at Kurt. "Frying itself."

"Does the Ghost field filter out smells?" Kurt said. "Because if it does, don't take it down until we're far away." He swallowed hard and finally turned to me, gesturing out at whatever was going on in the air that I couldn't see. "The arm of that thing keeps slapping at the shield, and there are all these sparks and flashes and flames, and chunks of it kind of crisp and shatter, and other chunks of it melt, and it's waving around like some Japanese rubber suit monster movie squid and there's smoke and puddles of slime --"

"Melting away." Jane gestured down at the ground. "It's in puddles, but they're shrinking. Hopefully the battle is taking place in another dimension or phase of reality, and it's not touching our reality, because yeah, disgusting."

"But you guys are the only ones who can see it. I'm here inside the field with you, and I can't see it," I offered.

"Good to know," Kurt muttered. He exhaled loudly. "And there it goes, finally retreating back into its lair. I really hope that thing wasn't hiding there in the shadows last year, when you and Pete had that trouble. The thought of it waiting to pounce on you..." He shuddered.

"If it wasn't, then when did it show up? If it was ..." I really didn't want to stretch my brain to try to explore all the options and possibilities.

We reported to Angela and Stanzer, and we agreed it was time to get some authorities involved. Meaning we went to Gordon, and he helped us come up with a believable story that was pretty close to the truth, to go to Chief Tanner. We needed authorization to have this PI, Simon Jones, followed. And set up surveillance on the flower building. According to official records, no one was renting the place. The owner was trying to declare it abandoned property and let Cutterville take it for back taxes. Problem: doing so would damage his credit score and generate all sorts of legal and business and financial repercussions. He couldn't rent it, couldn't sell it, and anyone who came to look at the property sometimes didn't even get out of the car to get a closer look. It was like the place was haunted, in the owner's own words.

Well, we knew the truth now, or at least part of it, but we couldn't tell anyone, could we?

And that cloudy, oily, churning fog of nastiness was sitting there right on the border of Neighborlee, watching the high school, watching anyone who came down Overlook Drive, anyone who entered our town. We thought things were bad with that weird house on the border of Darbyville and Neighborlee.

What was worse? Having two enemies watching us from different spots, waiting for a weak spot to form in the shield, to let them in? Or having one enemy watching from two strongholds?

"We need to perform an exorcism," Ford Longfellow said just an hour later, during our brief meeting of the guardians at Divine's. "The question is if we have the authority to do so, outside of our territory. And if we do, exactly how do we go about it?"

We couldn't have people watching the building 24/7, because for one thing, having people sitting so close to school property was going to make the school security, teachers, students, parents and the police edgy and suspicious. And second, we didn't have enough people who were sensitive to the flow of energy, to see or sense when something got active, to stand watch in regular shifts. We settled for regular check-ins, every few hours, depending on Kurt and Jane, Ford, and a couple of the Sheridan people. I was more sensitive to energy, but everyone voted me down when I put my name on the lists, since I had had several encounters with doppelgangers and Kerri, and they had seen me with Dawn. I was on their radar, though we had no idea to what depth or intensity.

We put the property and a "questionable situation" on the prayer chain at church. The fact that some of our friends knew about the whole weirdness last summer with Pi Surprise added extra energy to the protective and defensive prayers.

So it really shouldn't have surprised us that we hit the jackpot after only three days of sentinel duty.

Jones showed up at Stanzer's before office hours on the following Monday. Fortunately, Dawn had already left for school, driven by Bethany, who had volunteered for bodyguard duty to test her growing sensitivity to magic. For extra help, Maurice was riding with them.

The PI seemed agitated, and he even asked outright what time school started and if Stanzer knew what door the "poor runaway" would probably go through when she went to school. Stanzer couldn't decide if Jones was grasping at straws or he knew Dawn lived in the apartment on the top floor, and was just trying to catch him in a lie. Stanzer responded that he seriously doubted a runaway teen would turn herself in to the authorities and go to high school. Jones seemed surprised by the idea, and then flustered. He finally gave up fishing for answers and left the office, complaining about a headache and his eyes fogging up.

Ford had the morning shift watching the flower shop. Simon Jones pulled into the parking lot less than ten minutes after Stanzer sent out the alert to all of us that the PI was in town, and likely to settle somewhere to watch the high school. If Jones went after me to find Dawn, I was ready to hide in the back rooms of the newspaper office. Daniel was on duty, just in case we needed his immunity talent to help me. Although up until this point, Jones hadn't displayed any sort of special, magical gifting.

Well, the contrary PI turned down Overlook, and then passed the school entirely. Ford identified his car and watched him as he drove down the street running between Neighborlee and Cutterville. Jones never turned his head left to look at the high school. The lot could have been empty, for all the attention he paid to it. He pulled into the rutted, snow-filled parking lot of the old flower shop.

Ford hadn't seen any sign of the black fog that Kurt and Jane and even I had seen, up until that point. Then he said the air around the old building seemed to congeal and darken. He watched the dirty windows and boxy architecture transform into a sleek, modern, one-unit office building by the time Jones parked and opened his car door. The broken asphalt of the parking lot shifted and blurred and became black and solid, wet with melting snow. Jones never reacted, although Ford had seen his car bounce through a couple potholes.

For good measure, Ford snapped photos with the camera in his phone. When he was looking through the lens of the screen, he saw the building, minus the churning streaks of black fog that surrounded everything and reached out tentacles to pull Jones into the building. When we looked at the pictures he snapped later, we only saw the old building. That was pretty powerful magic at work, but at least we had the assurance it had some holes in it. It fooled Ford's eyes, but not the electronics of the camera and phone.

A big, elegant sign with fancy scrollwork proclaimed it a lawyer's office. That was a new tactic of Kerri and her minions. If this really was Kerri at work. If Asmondius' theories and the things Harry had told us before he went researching were true, this was old magic, rebellious Fae magic, something the Fae Realms and their modern-day leadership hadn't dealt with for centuries. Again we had the conundrum: be relieved we had only one enemy instead of having to deal with several on different fronts, or worry that the enemy would throw something new at us we weren't ready to handle?

Chapter Eight

Ford even made a note in his running report that we needed to add another layer of prayers to the defenses. He stayed on the Neighborlee side of the street, partially hidden behind the high school sign, and watched through binoculars as Jones went into the building. It occurred to us later that these people were expending a lot of energy to make the illusion realistic enough that anyone driving by could see the transformed building, and see the business taking place there, thanks to floor-to-ceiling windows. That made absolutely no sense, because anyone who went down this side street regularly would know what belonged there: a derelict building and broken-down parking lot. Who wouldn't freak out if they saw an elegant, remodeled office building that hadn't been there even an hour ago?

More sloppiness on the part of the enemy. These people, if they were *people*, were kind of stupid. They just didn't think things through. And what kind of idiots wasted that much magical energy, propping up an illusion so everyone passing by could see, and yet didn't expend the energy to fool electronics?

Enemies who didn't do their homework. Didn't know electronics? Maybe more proof of Harry's theory, that these were ancient Fae, exiled to a sideways dimension? Maybe having no contact with Humans until recently? So they were just winging it and doing the best they could in this new battle they had declared?

Were we supposed to feel sorry for the creepy morons? Umm … nope. Not after the nasty things they had done to my folks and had tried to do to me and Pete, and were doing now to Dawn, and the whole evil twin and doppelganger mess. No sympathy.

Through the gray-tinted glass wall, Ford watched Jones shake hands with several people in black business suits, and sit down in what looked like a conference room. His binoculars were fooled completely by the shrouding, disguising magic. Ford watched and dictated notes into his phone of what he was seeing.

A door appeared in the solid wall on the far side of the

conference room, which happened to be an outside wall. Five seconds later, it opened. Kerri stepped through. Ford knew what she looked like. He had been there last summer when we pulled Mum and Pop through the time window. He had seen Kerri approaching the beach, riding in a cloud of churning blackness.

This Kerri looked a good twenty, maybe even thirty years older than she had last summer, according to Ford. Her face was thinner, lined, the bones sharper, her eyes bigger and blacker. She was dressed elegantly and severely, in all black, and her hair was pulled back in a severe style. She scowled at Jones and the man shivered visibly.

Kerri stalked up to him, her mouth moving. Black fog swirled around her. Ford wasn't able to read lips, so there was no chance of knowing what she said. Jones went white and he slumped in his seat. His hands and shoulders shook as he tried to talk. Kerri grew taller, so her head was nearly scraping the ceiling of the room. Then she slapped him and sent him flying across the room. Through the glass wall. To land in the snow-filled parking lot. The lawyer-types in their business suits faded into more of Kerri's black-dressed minions with blurry faces. They picked up Jones and put him in his car. He looked like he was out cold. Then the black fog swirled around and the lawyer office melted back into the decrepit, should-have-been-torn-down-years-ago flower shop.

Ford was on the phone, reporting all this to Stanzer, when Jones woke up and pulled out his phone. Stanzer said he had an incoming call -- from Jones. As he reported to us later, Jones said his employer was distressed and upset that he had had the "bad sense " to make contact with a "rival, possibly unreliable private investigator," and if he didn't produce results soon, he would be fired. With prejudice.

Yeah, we shuddered at those last two words, when Stanzer said them. And we were safe inside the walls of Divine's Emporium when he told us. Jones wanted to meet. He sounded desperate, and afraid. He wanted to warn the runaway girl about the woman who was looking for her, and find out her side of the story.

Well, duh, that sounded like a fishing expedition to the rest of us. Stanzer didn't trust the man, knowing what had just transpired at the evil Fae-possessed flower shop. Either Jones was being controlled, or he had been scared enough to be a sloppy liar. When

Jones asked him to pick a place for a meeting, he made the mistake of saying he hoped Stanzer would welcome him.

That set off warning bells. Stanzer told Jones to pick the time and place, and he would be there. They went back and forth several times, with Jones trying to get Stanzer to choose, and Stanzer throwing the ball back into his court. Finally, Jones sounded like he was about to burst into tears, and said he was coming to the office. Stanzer only responded that he would be waiting. Then he got up and put his coat on, and stepped outside.

If Jones wanted to be welcomed into the office, and thereby into the building where Stanzer and Dawn lived, after Kerri had scared the fewmets out of him, then inviting him inside, welcoming him, was the worst thing to do. Stanzer had read all the right books, growing up, and had learned a lot of lessons in dealing with magical and cursed and enchanted people and creatures. Even if most of the stories were a lot of claptrap made up to really confuse Humans and keep them from seeing the truth, according to Maurice, it was better to be overly cautious.

Jones never showed up. Ford was still sitting half-hidden by the high school sign, and watched as the man's car just died, every time he tried to turn and drive on the Neighborlee side of the street. Fortunately, it wasn't a busy street, because his car blocked the eastbound lane. Several people stopped to help him push his car back into the flower shop lot. His car started up again without any problem, and he could drive it just fine. *Until* he pulled out into the street and tried to turn left, to go west. The engine died as soon as the front of the car crossed the double yellow line, entering Neighborlee.

Finally, Jones turned east, staying on the Cutterville side of the street. Ford got out of the parking lot as fast as he could, to follow him. Jones tried to turn left at the next street, running behind the Neighborlee Schools property -- and his car died as soon as he tried to cross the double yellow line. This went on for nearly an hour, until Jones stayed on the Cutterville side of the road and kept going. He called Stanzer to say he wasn't going to be able to make it, he was experiencing car trouble that he just couldn't explain. Could they make a meeting for later? Stanzer agreed, still careful not to invite the man into Neighborlee.

Jones called him on Wednesday and declared he had decided

to give up the case and take a vacation. He feared he was having a breakdown.

We weren't sure if Kerri had "fired" him and set him free from whatever control she had over him, or if he was running away and trying to put on a brave face. One menace had been removed, but was that a benefit or a drawback, since we had no idea who Kerri was going to use next?

And how did all this tie together, if it tied together, with the doppelgangers? What did Kerri want from Dawn and Bethany? Dawn couldn't skip school, but it was a fairly simple matter for her to use the doors on the other side of the building, keeping it between her and whoever crouched in the flower shop, watching the high school. We took it in rotating shifts to pick her up and drop her off at school when Stanzer wasn't there.

And we waited for Kerri and the doppelgangers and whoever or whatever was targeting Dawn and the rest of us, to make their next move.

~~~~~

Keep in mind, all this weirdness happened just in the first three weeks of January. I think Doni was the one who remarked that all this was Athena and Wallace's fault, because they had set a date for their wedding at long last, and the universe was marshalling its forces to ensure they didn't make it to the altar. She was trying to be funny, and we did sort of laugh a little when she said it. We laughed more when Athena suggested they just wave the white flag of surrender and elope, and Wallace panicked and insisted they had to have a huge, fancy blowout wedding, because his relatives would never forgive them.

We shouldn't have laughed, and we should have taken Doni a little more seriously. The universe was listening, or at least some of our enemies were close enough to hear us and take up the challenge.

None of us were sure that we didn't feel a shivering sensation of impending trouble, a creeping feeling up the spine. We could have, but with all the weirdness going on, how could we tell when the "uh oh" factor increased by a small percentage, compared with the current "oh, heck" feeling looming in the air?

We had more proof that the enemy was using really old magic, and they had been laying the foundation for their attacks since the
~~~~~

moment Dawn sent up that signal flare of Hunt energy in October, when she rescued those kids from Bidenski, the high school bully. What happened next had been a long time in the works, since fall, and made us wonder what other long-term plans of the enemy still waited to unfold.

To understand the long-range planning that went into the next attack, which wasn't triggered by Jones's failure but was probably meant to coordinate with his infiltration into Neighborlee, I need to relate some background.

As part of the expansion of services at Eden, our community center, we had added a Senior Center, a daycare and nursery school, and were working with an experimental program, the Homeschool Hub. This would allow parents who preferred homeschooling to bring their kids together for physical education and art classes and shared field trips. Essentially, this gave them the socializing that anti-homeschool people cited as their main reason for refusing parents the right to choose how and what their children were taught.

The Homeschool Hub program had the support of school choice advocates, and people who supported school choice if it didn't include handing funds over to private schools. I always wondered why people kept insisting it was "unfair" to give parents *back* the money they paid in taxes for education, so their children could be educated as they chose and not as the state and the increasing number of wacko extremists dictated. It was their money. Shouldn't they be allowed to spend it on their own children?

What was I saying? Yeah, "experimental" meant the programs offered by Homeschool Hub were being slowly phased in around the country as different community groups could pay for them. That meant supplies, equipment, and people to administer the programs. Our new Hub Coordinator had just arrived after the holidays, and had been settling in, preparing for the first organizational and orientation meeting to take place in the newest renovated room in the former Bucksby Factory, now the Eden Community Center.

Wednesday, I picked up Holly when she got off from the library. We stopped at Divine's to pick up Maurice, and headed over to Eden for the meeting. Holly was representing the library and Conrad had asked me to represent the *Tattler*. We picked up Charlotte Longfellow. She was representing the Neighborlee School System, even though she had retired from teaching just before Doni came to live with the Longfellows. I should note here that the Neighborlee school teachers supported the Homeschool Hub program. No national union full of elitists and troublemakers was going to tell them what to do. Neighborlee teachers had their own union. Plus the Neighborlee vibe of "go away, we don't like you and we don't want you here" helped get rid of troublemaker teachers. No law could force them to submit to being swallowed up by other unions. I belonged to the Neighborlee Teachers Cooperative when I was a teacher. We were constantly harassed by the national groups, insisting we were giving our students a sub-par education because we didn't let the national groups inflict their choice of curriculum on us. Yet Neighborlee Schools always tested in the top 10 percent across the state. Go figure.

On the way to Eden that afternoon, Charlotte hit us with a few minor bombshells. She had printouts of information on the coordinator, Leo Fidelus, that Athena had assembled after repeated requests for his background and other data were met with, "You'll find out all that at the meeting." That sort of runaround was always a warning sign of someone hiding something messy or dangerous. Athena proved once again just how good she was at piercing the walls and baffles and misdirection.

Leo's social media profiles weren't like a lot of scammers who contacted me on the social media sites, asking me to friend them, and the only pictures on their profile were of themselves, all updated in the last five hours. Leo's profiles went back eight or nine years, but were skimpy. He posted jokes and inspirational quotes, but nothing personal. Some of that was common sense and caution. After all, he worked with children, from kindergarten through high school, and even one picture of a child who wasn't a blood relative could raise suspicions.

Still, even if he couldn't talk about his career, didn't he have a personal life to feature on his social media profile? All the photos of Leo, what few there were, managed to be slightly out of focus. Every single one. In this day and age of computerized cameras designed to make it almost foolproof to get a clear picture, how did he manage that? Use a camera with a dirty lens?

More suspicious: Leo rented a house in Darbyville, on the same street as the house that gave us so much trouble when I was in college. Every time he listed the house number in his data, it changed. None of those numbers were legitimate addresses, yet nobody caught it until Athena compiled the information.

I already didn't like the guy, and that was before I learned he claimed the list of houses and apartments for rent in Neighborlee, which Gina at Eden had put together to help him with his move, hadn't helped at all. None of those vacancies were suitable. Athena made a note on that report that she was going to ask Gina for the list of addresses and vacancies, because her own sense of "something ain't right here" insisted the chances of every house and apartment being unsuitable were too small to be valid.

We drove to Eden hoping for justification for our uneasy feelings, or valid excuses for the oddness, because Leo Fidelus came highly recommended by the last few schools and communities he had worked with. The people at Homeschool Hub, some of whom I had interviewed last spring, were people I respected. Colleen, their leader, had even come to town and passed the Divine's Emporium test.

Colleen was in the lobby when we rolled and walked into Eden. The glass doors were fogged up from the icy weather outside and warm air inside and constantly opening and closing to admit business owners and educators and community leaders. She glowed, excited about this official launch of the partnership with our town and the opportunities for the children.

However ... she looked right at me and didn't even blink or react when she reached out to shake my hand and welcome me to the meeting. She greeted Holly and Charlotte the same way, as if they were total strangers. She didn't react when she led us over to the table for registration, and to get our nametags.

Holly and Charlotte had registration and information packets waiting for them, but not me.

"Are you sure you were registered?" Colleen asked me, when she worked her way through the long box of nametags. They were in alphabetical order, so how hard would it be to find a nametag beginning with a Z? I was the only Z in the group coming this afternoon. The closest letter in the alphabet to me was Max Uranker, coordinator for the Pee Wee football and Little League baseball programs.

Felicity's Jake was handling security and hovering on the sidelines. After Colleen had gone through the box three times, he signaled for me to wait, and crossed the lobby to Gina's office. She came hurrying out a few seconds later, and verified that yes, I was registered.

"I made all the nametags myself. Plus, I went through the list and crosschecked nametags and registration packets with Leo this morning, and I know both of yours were there." Then she let out a "hmph," and bent over to push aside the black plastic cube tucked halfway under the registration table, serving as a wastebasket.

Gina stood up, holding something behind herself. She gave me that sideways look, with a slight lifting of the eyebrows, that she had started using ever since her two close calls with the Rivals. She had experienced enough Neighborlee weirdness to see some freaky stuff now. She couldn't see or hear Maurice yet, but she had started noticing other things.

I gave her a little shrug and roll of the eyes. What response could I give to her very obvious signaled question of: *More trouble?* Followed by a little wince, which I interpreted as: *Should I evacuate now or wait until neon green gas starts filtering up through the cracks in the floor?*

Then Gina turned so I could see the legal-size white envelope she held pressed against her hip, with my name written on it. Someone obviously had tried to throw it out, but was sloppy enough to miss the wastebasket and just slide it under the table.

Why was the word "sloppy" coming up so much in my thoughts and conversation lately?

Charlotte and Holly, with Maurice perched on her shoulder, headed down the hall to the meeting room. Two more Homeschool Hub workers were passing out literature and giving their sales pitches for different programs that businesses and community groups could participate in. Leo was waiting in the meeting room. Gina led me to her office to make a new nametag. She had plenty of blanks left over. Colleen still hadn't connected my name and face and wheelchair with that afternoon in the gazebo, watching kids coloring the pavement around the center of town with sidewalk chalk provided by Angela.

"Okay, I don't know if I'm just more paranoid than usual ... I might just be hyper because Reggie Grandstone was in here, trying to get at old documents, and insinuating that he finally had proof that the factory belonged to his family." Gina sighed and slammed the filing cabinet shut, and waved the nametag blank sheet at me.

"My folks have all the paperwork you need, if he's trying that lame gambit again. The guy must be desperate to prove himself, after all the embarrassment from chasing poor Doni." I watched her settle at her computer and lean over to slide the blank into her inkjet printer.

"Same old, same old, when it comes to the Grandstones." She tapped her way through creating a new nametag for me.

"So what were you starting to say about being paranoid?" I asked, after the printer tugged the blank down and shot my nametag out five seconds later.

"Something just seems off about all those people. I spent more than an hour giving them a guided tour when they were here in November, but they're just wandering around like this is the first time in the building. Skyler couldn't find the bathroom just around the corner from the room they're operating in."

"Don't shoot me," Jake said, leaning into the office. "They all have that dazed look in their eyes way too often. Makes me wonder if they've been gassed or sniffing something or basically doing things people who work with kids should not be doing."

He reached into his jacket and brought out a handy little breath and sweat sampler Kurt had been developing. It couldn't be used for court purposes and wouldn't be acceptable in legal proceedings for the simple fact that it hadn't been patented or tested or verified as reliable. But Jake liked to use it just to give himself a heads up in questionable situations.

"If you're asking for my permission, and my support if someone gets offended and sues us for invading privacy," Gina said, "go right ahead. Ensuring the safety of our kids is more important than anything else. Horace Carr even put that in writing for me, so Carr, Cooper and Crenshaw will support us."

"Uh … hate to tell you, but I already did my sampling. Those people haven't been doing anything except maybe too much sugar and caffeine. Nothing toxic, nothing synthetic I can detect, but they're clearly under some kind of influence." Jake gave me an apologetic little shrug. "I met those folks when they were here last time, and they might look the same and have the right ID, but they *aren't* the same people. Little ways. Subtle ways."

"So we've got robots taking their places?" Gina said with a creaky little laugh. Like she wanted so much for the idea to be a total joke.

It was a good thing I hadn't had much for lunch, too busy getting work done before I took off for the day. The Valentine's letters had started rolling in already, and I had been trying to choose the launching point for my first lecture on true love in my *Talk to Terry* column. If I had had my usual "Thank You, God, it's Wednesday and I can relax for half a day" lunch, I might have hurled it right there on Gina's clean office floor.

Doppelgangers? Could doppelgangers have taken over the entire Homeschool Hub team?

Yet how could they get into Neighborlee without coming up against that improved, constantly recalibrating shield? How could they get through without tripping the alarms?

"Call Gordon," I said, and didn't care if both Gina and Jake did it.

Gordon had become quite adept at coming up with stories that had enough truth in them for Chief Tanner to accept. It was a blessing and a benefit to have a local cop as support for the guardians.

"I'm going to call Angela." Then I should probably head outside and contact London or Sherwood. Either they had missed something, or our enemies were getting a lot trickier and smarter and had found a way through the shield.

Or had the shield gone down somehow, without our friendly AI's noticing?

No, I couldn't believe that.

"Hey, we got a problem," Maurice called, zipping into the office.

Chapter Nine

Maurice came in for a hard landing on my shoulder, at enough speed he nearly slid off. He grabbed hold with both hands, flattening his wings against his back, and pulled on the shoulder seam of my sweater far enough Gina would have freaked out if she saw it. Fortunately, she was reaching for the phone.

"What's wrong?" I half-whispered. I pushed my wheelchair hard with my brain, to get out from behind the counter and heading for the door, at slightly higher speed than was wise for such a confined space.

"That new guy, Leo?" Maurice settled down on my shoulder and caught hold of my earring for balance.

"What did he do?" I felt sick. What kind of a whammy was he putting on the people who were already in the meeting room?

"Nothing yet ... except the guy doesn't look like his profile picture."

"How?" I grabbed my wheels and skidded to a stop about twenty feet down the hall that would take me from the office to the meeting room. Most of the traffic had already headed into the meeting room, so there wasn't anyone walking past right that moment to hear me, or for me to get in their way.

"The printout Charlotte gave you guys, and the profile sheets he's handing out when people walk in the room? They don't look like him. Maybe the real Leo Fidelus looks like a tall, skinny GQ version of Leonard Hoffstedder with a receding hairline, but the guy standing behind the table has got a head of dirty blond hair and a beard full of crumbs that don't match the cookies he's eating, and he smells like he hasn't had a shower in five days, with a beer belly hanging over jeans that can stand up on their own. And nobody notices. I told Holly the guy smelled like a locker room and she said all she smelled was that green cologne you guys had to find, when you were shopping at Macy's."

"Did she shake his hand yet?" I asked, reacting entirely on gut instinct. I had an awful, momentary vision of everyone Leo came into contact with getting drugged, either by smelling whatever covered up the odor of dirty skin and hair and clothes, or by touching his hand.

"Heck no. As soon as I told her, Holly got herself and Charlotte out of line." Maurice hopped off my shoulder and flew in front of me now. He pointed at a room down the hall past the open meeting room door, with the lights off. Holly and Charlotte waited in the doorway. They waved to me. "Got to tell you, kid, the guy ... buzzes. It's not real strong. Not from where I could see him clearly. And that's the freaky part. From the doorway, he looks just like his profile picture. Kind of blurry, but Leonard, y'know? Then when I got close enough to smell him ..." Maurice shook his head and gave me a slightly nauseated frown. "It was like a whaddayacallit thing, like they had at the play where something was painted on it, but when the lights came up behind it, the scene went invisible?"

"A scrim. Like he was wearing an illusion, and it fell apart when you got close enough?" I shuddered and Maurice's nausea transferred to me. Part of that sick feeling was anger. This was getting irritatingly monotonous. Why did the creeps keep hitting my town and playing nasty mind games and throwing illusions at my friends?

Well, duh, I knew the reason for that. Neighborlee was a plug keeping the creepies and nasties from other dimensions from pouring through to invade. We were also the reinforcement ring on the filler paper of reality, keeping it from being torn loose of its moorings, and allowing the dangerous and creepy things of Earth to escape into other dimensions and realities. The guardians never signed on for this job, but it was ours, and we refused to let down our home, no matter what it cost us.

"About sums it up," Maurice said.

"Can I ask you to get closer, test this guy? See if he reacts to you, if he can sense you or even see you? Maybe find out the source of this buzzing? By now, Gordon should be on his way. Have Holly call Kurt and Jane, see if either of them can come over." I took a deep breath. "Maybe we should send for Angela, too. I'll do recon, even though I'm not the evil magic detector ... try to do something before they show up."

"Gotcha. I'll tell Holly to call, and I'll meet you in there." He zipped away, so fast I swore he left a trail of sparks from the speed of his wings, as he arrowed down the hall.

I took the time to pause and pray, one of those, "God, this is a mess, I don't know what we're going to need, but I trust You to come through," prayers. Then to save my superhero energy, I grabbed my wheels and pushed hard, heading for that doorway of doom and whatever or whoever waited in the room. I will not lie: I did not want to go in there. I had never felt more like the helpless little crippled lady than I did right that moment. I felt more vulnerable than I did the day before Christmas Eve when we laid that trap for Jay Parker and I was the bait.

Gina caught up with me about twenty feet from that door, and I told her to try to keep people from going in. That used up about thirty seconds. After what we had gone through last summer, Gina's knee-jerk reaction when I asked her to do something that didn't make sense was to just do it and wait until the dust settled to ask questions.

I moved another ten feet toward that doorway before Gordon hurried into the building and caught up with me. I had never been so glad to see the big, homely, incredibly sensitive and smart bruiser of a cop. He knew about Maurice and had met him on one of those days Maurice was full-size, visible, and audible. So when I said Maurice had detected something hinky about Leo Fidelus, and we had to investigate and head off trouble, Gordon just nodded and fell into step with me. No questions. Just a straightening of his shoulders and a determined set to his jaw. I made a silent promise to Mandy that I would do my best to send him home to her tonight without any folding, spindling, or mutilating.

Maurice had taken care of his errand and returned to the meeting room. I saw Holly and Charlotte both in the doorway, on their phones. Maurice zipped to the meeting room doorway to meet us as we entered. There was no one behind us in the hall, and the line of people meeting Leo had gone down to almost nothing.

"The guy's got something on his right wrist. Looks like some old coins, really old and dirty, with these glow-in-the-dark designs scratched into the dirt. It doesn't so much glow as it sucks up the light around it, every time he shakes hands with someone," Maurice reported, hovering in front of me.

My back kind of ached as I tried to figure out how he could fly backwards and stay far enough away I didn't go cross-eyed to keep him in focus.

"A dark streak, like a shadow, reaches out from his hand whenever he makes skin contact, and slides up under their sleeves," he added. "Don't let the guy make contact."

I passed the warning on to Gordon, keeping my voice low, and praying there was enough noise from chatter around Leo's table that he didn't hear what I said.

"I don't see anything," Gordon said.

That really didn't surprise me, but I didn't like it. Gordon's enhanced sensitivity had been proven time and again in tense situations. If he didn't see bracelet or shadow, that meant something was hiding them. Some kind of magic talisman? Charms?

But just because I couldn't see it didn't mean I couldn't touch it, and I wasn't thinking about physical touch. By the time I got to the front of the meet-and-greet line, I knew what I had to do.

Maurice let out a yelp when I reached out in response to Leo's outstretched hand.

Leo heard and looked around. He clearly didn't see Maurice, who was on the verge of dive-bombing to put himself between my hand and Leo's, but he could hear him.

I reached with all the focus of my mind, and then I could see the coins on Leo's wrist. They were just as Maurice described, dirty, with weird symbols scratched in the dirt, and a black light glow. I saw the shadow curl up and prepare to launch at me.

"Not gonna happen," I muttered, and gritted my teeth.

Leo shook his head, visibly confused by my words.

I yanked mentally as hard as I could, pulling those coins off his wrist, and flung them backward toward the door behind me.

Leo shrieked. The coins sparked, an ugly greenish-red color, like pus mixed with blood in a dirty wound.

He turned into … Ricky Casper. Sort of. I could see both faces, Leo Fidelus and Ricky, sort of wavering in and out, one over the other, like someone was trying to change a channel and kept sliding back and forth.

Nobody reading this knows that name, because I had tried for years to wipe it from my memory.

I had dated an earlier version of Ricky Casper, with shorter hair and cleaner aroma, in my early years of teaching. He pushed a little too hard and too soon to make our relationship "official," and I listened when gut instincts said to run away. He didn't pass the Divine's Emporium test because he refused to go inside, making excuses not to meet Angela. Then he got nasty when we broke up. I want to know how we could "break up" when we hadn't officially been together.

Gordon did some investigating at the time, because Ricky was so nasty to me. It helps having a cop as a buddy. Bottom line: Ricky was a wannabe pedophile, and he was trying to get close to me so I could give him access to the kids I taught, in school and Sunday school. More important, he wanted access to the kids I worked with twice a month at Neighborlee Children's Home, when we had alumni nights. One of my first warning signs was when he got upset that I wouldn't take him with me until he had been vetted by Mrs. Silvestri, who was still our lion at the gates at that time.

Now, just to be sure I wasn't hallucinating, because yeah, we had been under a lot of stress the last few weeks, I shouted, "Ricky Casper!"

He flinched and looked at me, and his eyes got big and his mouth dropped open. Then he recovered and offered this really lopsided smile and shook his head.

"What did you say?"

"I know it's you, Ricky." And now I knew what happened to my nametag and why my registration packet nearly hit the wastebasket. I hooked my thumb over my shoulder at Gordon, who had dropped back when I reached for that band of coins on his wrist. Where were those coins, anyway? "Gordon, you remember Ricky Casper, the creep I dated who had a thing for little girls and boys?"

"Yeah," Gordon growled, and even though I couldn't see him, I could feel him reaching for his gun. Or maybe just his handcuffs. "I do."

Gordon was my hero, because as I later learned, Maurice and I were the only ones at that time who saw the Ricky Casper face under the Leo Fidelus mask.

"Got it!" Maurice let out a yelp, and I heard the clatter of coins hitting the tile floor. "Don't got it! The thing burns like there's acid on it."

I guessed Maurice was trying to pick up the band of coins and fly away. He couldn't because they scorched him, reacting negatively to his inborn, if limited magic.

"What is that thing?" Ricky half-shrieked, pointing at Maurice.

"What thing?" Gordon said.

The other people around us were murmuring, and some pointed, and a few gave Ricky weird looks. Something about the double vision I was experiencing changed. The Leo image visibly faded and lost dominance. I hoped that whatever disguising magic he was using, it was wearing off now that he had lost contact with the coins. Ricky must have realized that, because as the mutters got louder and people backed away from the table, he looked around and then bolted.

Ricky barely took five steps before Gordon proved just why he was one of the best line tackles on the Neighborlee High School football team. Go Pikes! They hit that fairly new tile floor and slid a good ten feet, with Ricky shrieking and Gordon calmly catching hold of his flailing arms. Gordon would have made a champion wrestler, because he had the moves. He held Ricky flat despite his bucking and kicking and shrieking, until he got the handcuffs on him. Then he left Ricky writhing on the floor with his hands cuffed behind his back, doing the worm and getting nowhere no matter how much he flailed.

Maurice swooped in and got hold of a leather thong, which didn't sting him, and yanked another talisman from around Ricky's neck. He flew away, singing the Mighty Mouse theme, and brought it to Charlotte, who had a big handkerchief ready to take it. I took care of picking up the band of coins with my telekinesis while Gordon acted all official and asked everyone to leave the room.

Ricky, meanwhile, was having a seizure, writhing and foaming at the mouth and his eyes rolling back in his head. He didn't turn blue, fortunately, because I wouldn't have wanted to give him CPR, and wouldn't have wished that task on my worst enemy.

That was when Kurt and Jane flew down through the roof in the Ghost field. They materialized after everyone else had left the room. I held up the coins, still with my telekinesis.

"What do you see?"

Jane phased out until she was halfway transparent, and got close enough to the coins her nose almost touched them. "Like nothing I've encountered yet. Lots of layers to it. Some of them are trying to phase out."

"Charlotte has another one of those coins that he was wearing around his neck. Probably to buffer his disguise, or maybe it was mind control." I wheeled up close enough to get a good look at Ricky, who lay on his side now with his mouth open, eyes half-closed, and a big puddle of drool forming on the floor.

Gina came running to let us know Colleen and the other Hub ladies had all collapsed. Nobody lost consciousness, but they weren't sure where they were or what day it was. That supported the theory of mind control. Whether Ricky was just another dupe of the enemy or the one holding the reins, he was the focal point. When we pulled the plug by removing the coins, the link with and control over the three ladies of Homeschool Hub had been broken.

Maybe his brain got fried in the backlash, or maybe his evil masters punished him, because he didn't regain consciousness by the time the ambulance arrived. Gordon followed the ambulance to the hospital and called Chief Tanner on the way. Gina got everyone calmed down and came up with some cover story, while Charlotte and Holly and I took care of the three Homeschool Hub ladies. We couldn't fit all six of us into my Jeep, so Charlotte drove Colleen in her car, Holly and I took the other two ladies, and we went to Angela.

I had the coins wrapped up in some scarves Holly found in the Lost and Found at Eden, inside a plastic grocery bag, sitting in the console of my Jeep. Nobody wanted to touch those things. Maurice perched on Holly's shoulder, and she sat in the front seat. Every time I turned to look at him on the drive to Divine's, he was glaring down at the bag, like he expected something nasty to erupt out of it, and he was keeping it back by force of will.

"Uh ... Lanie? You smell anything?" he asked, when I made the right turn into the residential section around Divine's.

"Like what?" Then I sniffed. "Smells like --"

"Burning polyester," Holly said. She hit the button to open her window.

I looked down and saw gray smoke rising from the scarves inside the bag. I hit my window control, opening all the windows, and pulled over to the curb. Holly snagged the plastic handles and hit the door latch, but before she could jump out, Maurice yanked the bag from her grasp and darted outside, to drop the smoldering mess into the nearest snowbank. I got out of my Jeep, praying my legs wouldn't betray me without warning, and walked around to the curb. I slipped a few times once I stepped into the ankle-deep snow. The smoke vanished as Holly and I took turns shoveling handfuls of snow into the bag. Two of the scarves were polyester and had melted into a knotted mess. The third was wool and didn't show any scorch marks. After a little debating, we scooped snow around the coins and packed it into a ball, wrapped the wool scarf around the ball, the other scarves around it, and back into the bag.

No smoke erupted, and no water gushed out on the remainder of the drive to Divine's. Angela was waiting for us, standing behind her gate, wrapped in her peacock print shawl. Her mouth was pressed flat in a somber, worried expression that made her seem decades older. She braced herself on the gate and watched as we got out of the Jeep.

Charlotte had gotten there ahead of us, and since no one was in her car, parked on the curb beyond the gate, I assumed she and Colleen were inside already.

I lifted the bag with my mind, just to be on the safe side, and swung it through the air to approach the gate. It jolted and thrashed, getting more violent with every foot closer we got to Angela's gate.

Or maybe the violent reaction was to Angela herself.

She gestured and I dropped the bag on the sidewalk outside the gate. Angela stepped out and very slowly leaned over and tugged on the loosely tied handles of the plastic bag, untying them. The bundle of snow and scarves and coins jolted more fiercely, as if something alive in there was terrified. As soon as she let go, the bag turned over, spilling everything out, scattering snow everywhere, with a gush of steam. None of that made sense, because where did the steam come from if the snow wasn't melting?

The coins rattled and chimed, off-key, as they rolled out onto the salted flagstone sidewalk. Angela flinched and moved back a step, and she looked pale. Then she pressed her lips flat together and stepped back through the gate. For a second, I nearly thought she was running away, but she just went to retrieve a bottle of her detoxifying cleanser and purifier from where she left it on the porch. We had used the same stuff last summer when we had that problem with the magically intoxicated waters of Black Water Pool and Jinx's pond. Angela unscrewed the top of the bottle and poured it on the pile of coins.

They let out a shriek and leaped up high enough they nearly touched her face, where she was bent over to watch them. Before most of those coins hit the sidewalk, they evaporated in puffs of foul-smelling, greenish-gray smoke.

"Angela!" Maurice shrieked and darted forward as she swayed and took a few staggering steps backward.

Yeah, like he could catch her?

I ran, and my legs wobbled as I caught her, with my arms and my telekinesis. Angela's throat worked and she made a sound like she was going to heave. I had no idea what to do to help her. She clutched at me and took a few deep breaths, then she seemed to get herself under control again.

"I have never smelled anything so foul in all my life," she murmured, as she wiped her sweaty face with both her hands.

"I didn't smell anything, did you?" I turned to Holly. She shook her head.

"You're lucky," Maurice said. "A smell like that makes you want to heave your insides out." He snorted. "Worse than Vogon poetry."

It took me a few seconds to catch the reference. It was from *The Hitchhiker's Guide to the Galaxy*, where the poem was so bad the poet's own intestines reached up through his throat to strangle him and stop him reciting.

We all needed the moment of lightness, no matter how bad the joke. Especially when my legs decided they had done too much for the day. My knees and ankles turned to rubber and I was just a mass of uncomfortable tingles from the waist down. This time Angela had to help me stay upright while Holly hurried to get my wheelchair out of the back of my Jeep. Between us, we got the other two Homeschool Hub ladies into Divine's. Charlotte was just lifting the steeper from the huge pot of tea Angela had made to counteract whatever kept the ladies in a daze.

They were at least aware enough to hold mugs of antidote tea and drink for themselves, so we didn't have to help them. By the time we refilled their mugs, they were already coming out of it. As we started getting bits and pieces of the story, we got angry.

Colleen and her co-workers had been drugged and programmed, but only enough to be outwardly cooperative. Whoever the enemy was, they were nasty enough to leave the women conscious and aware of what was going on, but unable to resist. Someone else spoke through their mouths and someone else moved their limbs. Ever since they came to town to meet with Leo and begin preparing for today's meeting, and they discovered that Ricky had taken over his identity, they had been living in an awful waking nightmare. They acted as if everything was normal, all the while able to see through the Leo mask Ricky was wearing.

He was one of those villains who saw himself as a mastermind and bragged to his captive audience. From what the women recalled of his words, he thought he was important and powerful even while someone else was pulling the strings. He didn't realize he was just as much a prisoner as the women.

There was a real Leo Fidelus out there, but he had taken three months off to help his sister with newborn triplets. Ricky had targeted the women of Homeschool Hub because they had investigated his newest identity and shredded it to find the truth when he applied to work with them. He was out to punish them for denying him access to a new crop of victims. Just like he had tried to do to me.

Someone helped Ricky steal Leo's identity and gave him all his falsified documents, but the women had no idea who. While they sat in their office, unable to do or say anything outside their ordinary routine, Ricky had taken phone calls. Some had made him furious, and others had him terrified.

Angela was back to normal, just a little more quiet than usual, by the time Chief Tanner and Gordon showed up to talk to the women. She had enough time to supply them with a believable story: Ricky had used masks and makeup, and he had first drugged them and later threatened their families' safety if they didn't cooperate. It was a fragile story at best, but as we discovered, God answered a large handful of prayers that I hadn't really prayed yet. Ricky was in a coma. Chief Tanner had stayed in the ER long enough for the doctors to pronounce Ricky effectively brain dead, even if his body continued functioning. It looked like that last seizure when he fought Gordon had been the result of something bursting deep inside his brain.

So, one problem taken care of, a few questions answered, but no real, usable answers. The coins were gone, so Jane and Kurt hadn't no chance to examine them. Ricky wasn't about to give us any answers, even if he had wanted to cooperate, which I doubted would happen. The guy was a born liar and justified everything he did in relation to what would make him happy.

On top of everything else, Homeschool Hub was understandably reluctant to continue setting up in Neighborlee. They were grateful to have been freed from their captor and not at all sorry to hear he was the next best thing to dead.

We were back to square one, in a lot of ways. We had some clues to just how angry or determined or whatever our enemies were, but no clues to who they were or where they came from. This led back to Dawn, because Ricky had applied to Homeschool Hub right after the pictures were taken of me in the high school parking lot with Dawn.

Our enemy was desperate enough to react immediately. At least, we hoped that was desperation, with a large helping of arrogance thrown in.

That night, my evil twin walked into the comedy club in Rocky River where I appeared maybe once a month. Ramon, the owner, freaked out when he saw her. He was smart enough to call me for verification while two of his waitresses squealed and proved all that peroxide they used on their hair damaged brain cells. While they were demanding to know how I/she got her legs fixed, Ramon talked to me on the phone.

"Yeah, Lanie, how come I'm sitting here in my office looking at you, standing up and letting Terri and Chasity gush all over you?"

"Say what?" I felt sick. I must have yelled or something, and I must have looked as sick as I felt. The noise around me died down -- we were still in the social part of the planning meeting of our Star Trek club's officers.

"Yeah, somebody who looks just like you walked in here. Walked," Ramon emphasized.

"That's not me. I've got somebody pretending to be me and causing trouble. The skanky twit even knows I've got natural four-wheel drive." I gestured to Felicity for paper and pen.

While Ramon described what he had just seen, I scribbled the address and wrote in big letters, **Call Kurt. Evil twin strikes again.**

Felicity let out a couple dozen sparks when she saw that. She hadn't lost control of her EM bursts since the big showdown with the oil slick monster just after New Year's two years ago. She hurried out of the meeting room with her phone -- something she could have now that she had her electronic surges under control.

Then I had to conduct the meeting. With all those questioning and concerned looks focused on me, I had to give some explanation. I basically told the truth, just not all of it.

"There's some jerk running around, pretending to be me, and walking into places where I usually go. Freaking people out, seeing me up on my own two feet. Except of course, that isn't me. Hey." I looked around the room, getting that little shiver of inspiration. "If you guys see anybody who looks like me, don't do anything stupid, because she has to be kind of psycho to be playing a trick like that. But get pictures or something and call me, call Gordon, document what's going on, okay?"

Knowing our club's officers, with all the different extremes of creative and wacky, word would get around town a lot faster than if I had taken an ad out in the *Tattler*. The sooner people knew someone was wearing my face, the less harassment I would run into from people who would see me in my chair and accuse me of faking my condition to get a prime parking space. It was bad enough I regularly ran into people who insisted that if I could drive, I didn't need my handicapped parking card. Who put them in charge?

It takes all kinds in this world, but couldn't we take some of those kinds and send them to another planet?

Of course, maybe I was just in a bad mood because it wasn't even February yet, but I was being deluged with idiotic Valentine's letters for the *Talk to Terry* column.

Chapter Ten

February. One of the gloomiest months of the year. Just when people are starting to come out of shock from their Christmas credit card bills, merchants have a way to induce people to spend more money.

Look at this sample of the letters I anticipated having to read and answer in the coming four weeks. Actually, six weeks, because while there were four weeks until the torture of Valentine's Day shopping and sweethearts angsting was officially over, I always got dozens of letters from bozos who wanted my advice on how to make it up to their girlfriends for forgetting to do anything, and from girls who tortured themselves with the question of whether to take the oblivious dweeb back. Seriously? To the first: how could they not know Valentine's Day was coming, with all the advertising and red hearts and lace everywhere they looked since before the Christmas decorations were put away? To the second: the answer is no. Always no. As in "Don't let the door hit you on your cheapskate behind on the way out."

Dear Terry:

Could you put out a general letter to girls advising them that nagging their boyfriends to remind them Valentine's Day is coming up is not a good way to keep that boyfriend?

My girlfriend is really making me have second thoughts about how smart it was to get back together with her a few weeks ago. She keeps making comments about how I broke up with her just before Christmas to avoid having to give her a present. That was a for-real fight! I just didn't appreciate her dragging me all over the state doing Christmas shopping. Okay, maybe I wasn't diplomatic or sensitive when I griped about the jerks in her family who sure didn't deserve any presents other than a restraining order, to make them shut up. Nothing like constant criticism from people I don't like anyway to make a guy seriously consider breaking up so I never have to spend any more holidays with them. Thanksgiving was torture, you know what I mean?

She accused me of manufacturing most of the fight, and then told me her sisters and their husbands were all right about me. What guy likes to hear that?

So yeah, I stayed away for two weeks before Christmas, and nearly forgot about our plans for New Year's Eve. We had reservations for this really great package, and we couldn't cancel at the last minute. And she claimed I only went because the party center wouldn't refund the money to me because she made the reservations with her credit card. Mine was over the credit limit, but that was back in November.

So that brings us to Valentine's Day coming up. She expects me to go all out to make up for ditching her so I didn't have to buy her a Christmas present.

Maybe breaking up permanently is the best choice. Except I still owe her for the New Year's tickets, and she's got this one brother-in-law who will take it out of my hide if we break up and I haven't paid her back yet. Know what I mean?

What do I do? How come girls put a price tag on things? Why can't a guy just say, like once a week, "Hey, babe, you know I love you, right?" and that's enough?

Penniless and Puzzled

Dear Penniless:

"Hey, babe, you know I love you, right?" has been used way too often by guys to get themselves out of trouble, when their actions say the opposite way too loudly.

If the problem really is money, and your lack thereof, you can still put shoe leather on your feelings. The effort you make goes a long way toward making up for price tags. Take her for a romantic drive. Go for a snowy walk at the zoo. Cuyahoga County residents get in free on Mondays. Bring her a cup of her favorite coffee when you meet up at school, or take it to her at work. Leave her mushy notes on her email and texting. Post pictures of her with lots of hearts on them on social media. Time spent on making someone feel special is a lot more valuable than money. Any bozo and brute can spend mega-bucks on jewelry and candy and flowers and then go right back to abusing or neglecting their victims.

This newspaper regularly lists inexpensive and free things couples can do for Valentine's Day. I guarantee, being a girl myself, she won't care that you used the list. It's the fact that you actually did something.

If you do anything at all.

Her relatives don't like you because they see you care more about your wallet than her. If you prove them right by breaking up with her again to get out of doing something for Valentine's Day, don't even think about making up with her after February 15. That's a pretty transparent ploy, and a bad habit to get into.

If you don't invest some time and creativity into the relationship -- notice I didn't mention money or presents? -- you'll get a reputation. Pretty soon no girl, no matter how desperate, will want to invest her time and feelings in you.

First, find a way to pay back what you owe her. Then make up your mind whether to hold onto the relationship. And remember what I said about the list of inexpensive and free romantic things to do.

Terry

Dear Terry:

This is my fourth draft of my letter to you. The funny thing is, I'm pretty sure what you're going to say, but I still need to write and make sure I'm not being a doom-and-gloomer.

I think my boyfriend is getting ready to break up with me. Again. We broke up just before Christmas. I was stupid and went out and bought his present anyway, and then returned it on Christmas Eve. I figured if he hadn't made up with me by then he hadn't bought me anything. Which is kind of pitiful, because our whole argument was about getting presents for people he thought weren't worth it. I felt like his attitude was affecting me.

I didn't enjoy New Year's Eve, because he made up with me to use the tickets for a big blow-out night that I had to buy on my credit card because he's constantly going over his limit. He still hasn't paid me back, but I've heard him boast to his friends about the big fancy New Year's Eve he gave me. How did he give it to me if I paid for it? Now I'm getting the same antsy feeling I had just before our big fight during Christmas shopping.

Am I wrong or right, to expect him to break up with me to avoid buying me anything for Valentine's Day? And am I wrong or right to feel like relief is stronger than the headache whenever I think about breaking up and staying broken up?

He's not really my boyfriend, is he?

Please tell me I'm not as big a loser as I feel like I am?

Reality Check in Rocky River

Dear Reality:

See the previous letter in this column. Honey, I feel for you, and I cheer for you. It hurts, but you're already halfway down the path of healing and freedom.

If you think he cares more about money than you, and can't make any effort to do inexpensive things that make you feel special, do you really want to spend even the next few weeks with him? The rest of your life is out of the question, of course.

Say you're right, and he breaks up with you to save on Valentine's candy. Say you take him back. What are the chances he'll break up with you before Sweetest Day, your birthday, and any holiday that requires or implies an exchange of some token of affection?

Yes, some of the guilt should be laid at the feet of the greeting card and candy companies and jewelers and florists who conspire to create holidays where guys are made to feel like selfish jerks if they don't fork out a certain amount of money, and girls are brainwashed into thinking Snuggle Bunny doesn't really care if he doesn't fork over something.

Decide if this guy is worth the headaches now. If not, let him go, and consider yourself lucky. You dodged a bullet.

But here's a thought. Sit down and talk with the guy. Find out if money is the problem, or something else. I don't know how many books I've refused to finish reading, where the problem between the hero and heroine could have been solved on page 50 if they just sat down and talked. Instead, they angst and whine and worry themselves into headaches and binge on ice cream or beer. I hate books like that. Don't be like those people.

Terry

February is a big, busy month for the *Tattler*, with several editions chock full of Valentine's greetings that take up five or six pages, in the two issues before and two issues directly after Valentine's Day. Why after, you might wonder? Well, to give groveling time to all the guys who missed the boat, despite the deluge of advertising. Most of our personal ads the edition after Valentine's Day were along the lines of "I'm scum, I don't deserve you, please forgive me and let me take you on a Caribbean cruise to make up for it." That sort of thing. Yeah, the flower and chocolate people, and the jewelers, made out big with the guilt trip shopping in the days following Valentine's Day, too.

Monday, January 24, three weeks before V Day, Daniel personally delivered the first onslaught of letters asking Terry's advice: a stack of letters four inches thick, sandwiched between two Godiva heart-shaped boxes of chocolate.

I got the strangest panicky feeling in my stomach when he walked into my section of the *Tattler* office and dropped his burden on my desk. Part panic, part sugar shock just from the aroma that seeped through the cardboard and silk and gold foil and cellophane. Part from the glee in his eyes. Part terror that he had bought chocolate for me. Sure, candy is one thing, but candy in a heart-shaped box, no matter what time of year, has dangerous implications that can't be avoided. Even if that candy had a "half-off" sticker on it in the weeks after V Day, there are always dangerous pitfalls and emotional traps that must be navigated with extreme caution.

And people wonder why I always say I prefer to celebrate Valentine's Day the traditional Italian way: go to a garage in Chicago and shoot someone. *(ba-da-dum!)*

If Daniel was going to bribe me, I would have been happy with a bag of Dove dark chocolate Promises. Regular shaped, not hearts, please?

"Terry has some major fans," he said, dropping into the chair in front of my desk. "Somebody has a problem big enough to try bribing you with chocolate."

Again, my stomach twisted and did a full-gainer. I felt all the blood leave my face, when it occurred to me that amid all that panic turning to relief, I felt a little disappointment that the chocolate *wasn't* from Daniel after all.

A definite sign I was getting sick. Along with realizing that I hadn't seen much of him since all the panic and weirdness at New Year's, and then with my evil twin visiting the Independence office. I missed his harassment. Other than funny little notes when he forwarded me the Terry letters he wanted me to answer for that week's edition, we hadn't had much contact at all. And I did miss him. As a friend. He had been majorly busy with the fallout from that tunnel and the doppelganger problem, after all. And that was with all the gifted people in the Sheridan group who were working on figuring out who was our new enemy. London and Sherwood hadn't come up with much of anything, and either the doppelgangers hadn't managed to decode the changing frequency of the shield and get back into Neighborlee to make trouble, or they had but were too tired from the effort to cause trouble. Neither option was very comforting. So yeah, everybody was busy, on the alert, and we just didn't have much time to socialize.

"Am I going to regret looking at all that?" I said, gesturing at the stack of letters and boxes of candy. I wasn't sure if I meant the candy or the letters or both.

"There's some pitiful stuff in there. I suggest you answer a couple of the sincere, pitiful ones in one issue, and then lambaste the morons with all the sarcasm you can muster in the other. Don't mix them." Daniel shook his head. "Some people just don't deserve sympathy. I mean, yeah, I'll agree that testosterone does cause brain damage, but these guys … their stupidity is self-inflicted, know what I mean? You could write out a rule book for how guys are supposed to treat girls, and make them read it, and they still wouldn't have a clue. Roast 'em for me."

"Your sisters raised you right."

He burst out laughing and slumped a little more in that stupid, uncomfortable chair facing my desk. "Sisters and nieces. I'll tell them you said so."

And with that, and his normal grin, whatever had felt wrong, poised on going into a really dangerous direction, had been shoved back into alignment. Thanks to all the Valentine's gush and mush, and yes, feeling a little jealous of all my friends who were happily married or heading for the altar, and the growing excitement over Athena and Wallace's wedding plans, well, things just felt a little unfair around me lately. Which made no sense. I just had to blame it on the insanity in the air that always came in February. I needed to find that passage in one of the epistles where Paul says it's good not to marry, and remind myself of the narrow escape I had with Ricky Casper. Daniel was my friend. That was all. I had totally misinterpreted some of those looks he had been giving me around New Year's. I had to remind myself of that. Or start calling him the Evil Overlord whenever possible.

Looking at that stack of letters he left on my desk, when he got up to go talk to Conrad, it wasn't too hard to call him the Evil Overlord for the rest of the day and mean it.

Until ... for the first time in my life, I felt a shiver go through the background energy of Neighborlee, about 5 that afternoon, just as I was tapping the controls to shut down my computer. I sat up and looked around, half-expecting to see the lighting had changed, or maybe the furniture was slowly vibrating as an earthquake built up enough force to be felt.

Nothing had changed outside me. Nothing rattled or moved out of position anywhere in the office. At least, as far as I could see. Just this momentary flicker inside me.

Not a sense of trouble, but a sense that something had sort of slipped around, changed position. And as I realized much later that night, after everything had been discussed and analyzed and I could look back, it wasn't the sense of something going wrong, but of something settling back into place where it belonged. Like when something was put back into place, but I never realized it was missing until moment. Mostly because it had been gone so long.

Don't worry if that doesn't make sense. It will in a little bit.

I reached for my keyboard to halt the sign out process, but the screen had already shifted to the powering down message. Sighing, I reached for my cell phone. I always preferred to talk to London on my big screen. There was no one in my section of the office to overhear, and I had had enough conversations with London, she was used to pretending to be Doni Longfellow if anyone walked over close enough to see and hear.

"Nothing wrong," London said, as soon as I clicked on the app -- yes, she and Sherwood had developed an app that would give us instantaneous contact with them. She laughed. "You're going to ask about that ripple in the shield and the boost in background energy. Aren't you?"

"Uh ... yeah. Boost? Like something good happened?"

"Someone drove through the shield ... ah hah, just getting the traffic camera and security camera signals. Lots of data running through the system at this time of day so even we get a delay ... yep, Col. Hayward, and it looks like he's driving to the Longfellows' house, and he has a woman in the car with him. Since the shield doesn't react that much when he drives through by himself, I'm going to hazard a guess the woman in the car is the one who upped the energy. Want me to keep track and report when I find out something?"

"Uh ... no. I think I'll just drive over there on my way home. Thanks."

"All part of our service." She winked at me, and I couldn't resist sticking my tongue out at her. She laughed, and the screen of my phone blanked.

I got to my Jeep, through the slush that had filled the parking lot and froze into ridges again with the drop in temperature as the daylight faded. I was folding up my chair to put it in the back seat when my phone buzzed against my hip. Umm, sorry, not dropping my chair right now. It kept buzzing while I closed the door and climbed into the driver's seat. The London and Sherwood app was flashing. That had never happened. Or maybe that was just because it had never needed to. I held my breath and tapped it open.

"Something big just tried to punch its way through the shield," Sherwood reported. "Fortunately, it bounced off and ran away."

"Singed and crying for its mama," London said, from off-screen.

Sorry, but I had to laugh at that. She was more and more her own person, yet at the same time borrowing a lot of personality traits from different members of the guardians. That was a heavy dose of me and of Athena on display just now.

Sherwood grinned and rolled his eyes. "It was following the path of the Colonel's car. It tried to go through at the exact same spot where he went through, like it hoped there would be a weak spot or even a hole. Definite reaction to the increase in energy. You need to get over there and warn them."

"Why can't you -- don't tell me, something is blocking reception on their phones, like before?" I bit my tongue against spilling a replay of a gripe session a few months ago, during a girls' night at Jane's place. We had been irritated by how our dependence on technology so often left us blind and deaf, because the enemy had found ways to keep us from communicating. The funny part that evening had been that London was griping just as loudly as the rest of us. Yes, London participated in girls' night.

"No, they're too busy hugging and talking and laughing. Nobody is paying attention to their phones or tablets." He shrugged.

"Do you know who the woman is?"

He shook his head. "We're a little busy buffering the shield and tracking whatever tried to punch through, to follow up on the facial recognition program."

"I'm on my way."

I had only gone two blocks when there was a thump on my roof, just as I stopped at an intersection. Kurt and Jane dropped through the roof to land in the back seat and passenger seat. At least they waited until I had stopped. Otherwise, I might have jerked the wheel, either into and up the curb or out into oncoming traffic. It was Neighborlee's version of rush hour, as people headed home from work. Granted, I nearly yanked my foot off the brake.

At least they waited until they were entirely in the car before becoming visible. I had to wonder what the people around me saw, or thought they saw, and what their reactions were. At least there were no crashes around me.

"Any news?" Kurt said, leaning forward so I could feel his breath on my neck. He had taken the back seat so Jane could sit up front with me.

"Have they ID'd the woman with the Colonel?" Jane asked.

"Whoever it is, everybody at Longfellows' is happy to see her." I looked both ways again, just in case someone had approached the other stop signs and since I didn't pull out right away, decided to cross the intersection.

"I meant the shield." Kurt slumped back in the seat.

"Why didn't you two go there, first?"

"We did. The best we can figure out is that the place where Hayward drove through is kind of fizzing, but a good fizzing, if that makes any sense," Jane said. "It's like there was a temporary patch and it's been replaced with the original material." She shrugged. "Again, if that makes any sense."

Actually, that did, but only after we had thought about it and looked back on the events of the last few hours. I arrived at the Longfellows' house just moments before Wallace pulled into the driveway. He parked crooked, slipped when he jumped out of his vintage Mustang, and nearly forgot to close the car door as he darted up the sidewalk to the front door.

"What's up?" Kurt called to him.

Wallace nearly slipped on the front step, and I guessed that he hadn't seen us getting out of my Jeep. "Doni called and said I had to get over here. I asked if it had anything to do with the shield fluctuation Sherwood just told me about, and she said she had no idea, but Athena was really happy and she needed me." He shrugged and lunged for the doorknob.

I fully expected the front door to be locked, and he would knock himself flat or sprain his wrist or something. The Longfellows usually used the kitchen door, but it was a shorter trip for Wallace from the driveway to the front door, than to go around the side of the house.

Ford appeared in the doorway. He was grinning so wide, his cheeks were red. My face hurt in sympathy for him. He stood back and gestured for Wallace to come inside, then stepped out onto the front step and watched us come up the driveway.

"Something going on with the town shield?" He didn't sound worried or even concerned.

Chapter Eleven

"Sherwood thinks it has something to do with whoever Hayward brought here," I said as we came up the sidewalk. "There was a fluctuation. I felt it this time, which means it has to be big. Then something tried to punch through at the same spot a short time after he drove over the border. London and Sherwood sent it packing, and hopefully slapped it hard enough it won't try again for a while."

"Ah." He nodded, his gaze going distant and thoughtful.

He offered me his hand to steady myself as I got out of my chair and navigated the steps. Today was one of my good days for my legs. Kurt carried my chair up the steps.

"Makes some sense, I guess," Ford said, as he guided me up over the threshold. "Considering Portia went away because of the vibes she was giving off, and we didn't want the Rivals tracking her or getting a clue how special Athena might be."

"Portia?" I admit I yelped the name, then the next second I saw her.

Portia Longfellow, sitting on the couch, with her arm around Athena, and Athena's arm around her. The resemblance between them was striking, now that they were together. Her face was thinner, the Longfellow wide cheekbones giving her sharp angles, and she had silver streaks in her dark red, short-bobbed hair, but she was a lovely promise for how Athena would be in thirty years. She was smiling up at Wallace and halfway to her feet to hug him when I spoke. Her eyes got big and she stared at me, but didn't pause in wrapping her arms tight around Wallace and then kissing his cheek. Her stunned look shifted into a smile.

"That's Athena's mother," Kurt explained to Jane, both of them right behind me. He grabbed my shoulder in one hand and guided me down into my chair.

Portia released Wallace and came over and bent down to hug me. "Thank you," she said, squeezing me tight. She smelled like sandalwood and sun-dried cotton and lemons. This close I saw the fine lines around her eyes and mouth. "For looking after my baby."

"She really didn't need it." My face got warm and I had the awful feeling everyone was looking at us, so I almost held onto Portia when she released me and stepped back.

"You know more clearly than anyone how much extra love a special, talented child needs," she said, shaking her head. "And I knew I could depend on you. I just hated knowing you thought I was a selfish, flaky little idiot who couldn't handle her responsibilities and --"

"No," I said, and flinched when Col. Hayward stepped into the living room from the kitchen, holding two cups of something steaming, and his gaze landed on me. "We know the whole story. You did what was right and best for Athena, for all of us."

"But until you found out, you thought I was a horrible mother." Portia shrugged. "It's all right. So did I."

"Mom." Athena came and wrapped her arm around Portia's waist. "Everything's all right now. Stop beating yourself up. I'm just so glad you're here now, and it's safe for you to come home!"

Now everything, well, *almost* everything, made sense. We settled down, and Wallace didn't look quite so uncomfortable as he had when we first came in. Everybody went for their cell phones when I told them about the second contact from Sherwood and London. Kurt had the sense to open the app and report to our watchful AI's, and identify the source of the extra energy that had come into Neighborlee. That was what it was -- Portia hummed, softly, just enough to set off a reaction when she came through the shield. That got a corresponding reaction from the doppelganger or its boss or allies or whatever. They must have assumed that any kind of change in the shield meant a momentary weakness.

London snickered, interrupting herself a couple times when she reported how the shield had strengthened now that Portia was inside the boundaries of Neighborlee. The doppelganger -- we really had to come up with a new name for this enemy -- had banged itself good and hard against the shield, and this time the shield had scorched it, instead of just bouncing it away. What were the chances the failed invader had a headache bad enough to discourage it trying to get into Neighborlee, or even impersonating me or Daniel any longer?

As soon as we had discussed what London and Sherwood had

found, and filled in missing information for each other, Kurt and Jane and I got out of there as soon as we could politely do so. This was family reunion time, after all. Portia needed time to settle in and figure out what she was going to do. She really was home to stay. With the changes that had strengthened the shield, Hayward had theorized, and Angela agreed, it would finally be safe for Portia to come home. Especially with the Rivals decimated if not totally destroyed. Besides, Athena needed her mother as she got to work planning her wedding. They had been deprived of so much during Athena's childhood and growing up years, they needed this memory together.

The idea to bring Portia home and keep it a surprise for the entire clan was entirely Hayward's idea. Right that moment, he was my hero. Especially when I saw how he took care of Portia. I had to wonder if there wasn't some emotional bond between them. Athena had been conceived through artificial insemination, because Hayward just wasn't the kind of man to cheat on his wife, even if it was for the purposes of deliberately conceiving a child who would carry on the Longfellow guardian heritage. Something had grown between them over the years, sharing stories about their daughter, reporting to each other every time Portia got a letter and pictures, and then later emails, or every time Hayward was in Neighborlee and stopped in to check with Ford and Charlotte. I kind of hoped, now that Portia was back in the country and Hayward had been a widower many years now, maybe they had a chance as a real couple.

Kurt, Jane and I immediately went to Divine's and caught Angela checking in on the family reunion via the Wishing Ball. She had a wistful sort of look on her face and blushed a little, but didn't really look guilty. I thought about teasing her that now we had her secret, how she was always on top of the things happening in town -- because she could spy on everyone. The words caught on my tongue. Common sense and gut instinct told me Angela wasn't a peeping Tom or voyeur or any of those nasty labels. She was watching because she cared, because she was happy for Athena and Portia.

We discussed the ripple in the shield, and Angela reminded us that Portia had a talent for feeling energy at work, so it would be wise to include her in our patrols and expand the network for guarding our town. With the return of stability in my legs and longer periods where they didn't tingle and shake and try to fold up under me, my ability to control my kinda-sorta flying had increased as well. Eventually, I might not need Kurt's help to go up in the sky and patrol. Maybe I could even put some controls on it, and do more than hover, or run, leap, and glide for long distances. We had been expanding our approach to flying patrol, including Jane enclosing us in our own personal bubbles of the Ghost field, so we could cover the width of several streets as we flew over Neighborlee. There was the distinct advantage of not needing our flying gear, since the Ghost field protected us from wind and rain and cold. We weren't limited to night patrols any longer, because the Ghost field kept us invisible. We also didn't need to dress in dark clothes and wear ski masks to hide our pale skin or hair. Kurt suggested that if Portia could feel energy at work, and follow it, maybe she could be on the ground, or driving and reporting in to us, while we flew overhead.

There was still the disadvantage of not having telepathic communication. Maybe the next generation would have that gift. Of course, by the time Wallace and Athena had children, or Felicity and Jake, or Kurt and Jane, maybe we wouldn't need phones or walkie talkies or telepathy, because communication gear would be implanted directly in our brains. Yeah, Kurt was working on that, but it was a long way in the future.

We split up and went home in pretty good moods, happy for Athena and Portia, with some ideas for the future, and optimistic about everything.

So we probably deserved the sleepwalkers, when they attacked.

To be fair, they didn't exactly attack. But it was a little creepy, on the edge of *Night of the Living Dead*, to see lone figures shuffling down the streets and sidewalks with glazed eyes and blank expressions, and not even shivering in the below-freezing late January weather. At least it wasn't snowing.

I hadn't gone straight home from checking in with Angela. I went to tell Mum and Pop about Portia returning to town and stayed for dinner -- not intentional planning or timing, but it was a dividend. Pete was living in the WBC dormitory, so the house was more quiet than it had been in years. We had a good time, remembering my childhood and all the time spent with Portia, her little quirks, her displays of brilliance. Looking back, we could see how her sensitivity to energy and the use of gifts had been affecting her actions and reactions and interactions with people. She didn't have the auditory signal that Kurt did, what he described as humming, and then the tingling sensation in his fingers to help him locate the presence and use of alien or otherworldly or just plain weird energy.

I stayed late, looking through yearbooks and newspaper clippings and home videos Mum and Pop pulled out, and just living in memories and the past. It was going on midnight when I finally left the family farmhouse and headed for home.

Looking back, I have to wonder how long the sleepwalkers would have been wandering the streets of Neighborlee, unnoticed, if I had taken Mum's suggestion to spend the night in my old bedroom. The sleepwalkers might have been walking for several nights already, rather than starting that night. Still, the fact that Portia's return had changed the pitch of the shield, the energy resonance, was more than a coincidence. Something had changed to make the enemy try new tactics. Or perhaps more accurately go into the next phase of their plan.

I took the back streets, which made for a shorter distance, but took longer getting to my place because I was doing twenty-five instead of forty, and there was a stop sign at every intersection. I was tired, which was part of why I took the back way, and I sometimes hallucinated a little when I was tired. So when I saw the lone figure shuffling down the center of the street, I took my foot off the gas, lowered the window a few inches to get some icy air in my face, rubbed my eyes, and blinked a few times.

It was still there. A wide-shouldered, hunched figure in a knee-length neon pink robe, Scooby-Doo print sleeping shorts and Cavaliers T-shirt, with what looked at first like a shower cap on his head -- except there were little sparkling lights under the cap. I found out later it was the newest hair restoration treatment gizmo on the market, with some revolutionary light therapy provided by the twinkling lights. Kurt looked them up and found out they were just ordinary Christmas tree lights with no special properties in them, no filters, no gamma rays or UV rays or anything like that. Total rip-off.

The shuffling figure was Mr. Cromwell. He lived three streets over from where I was driving. I knew his name and address all too well, from bad experience. One afternoon I stayed late at the *Tattler* after everyone else had gone home, and he came stomping into the office, demanding his newspaper. The problem was that he had subscribed to the Darbyville paper, but he was living in Neighborlee, one street away from the border, and there were no paper routes for the Darbyville paper that extended into Neighborlee. His newspaper had to be delivered by mail.

He came in on a Monday night, on a holiday, when there was no mail delivery. He insisted since he was a Neighborlee resident, it was the responsibility of our newspaper to make sure his paper was delivered, even though we didn't publish the one he wanted. I wanted so badly to know why he cared about the news in Darbyville when he didn't live in the town. When he first walked in, grumbling, he didn't say he was looking for the Darbyville paper. That would have saved us both a lot of time and changed my tactics. I took his address and told him I would give the information to the circulation office when they came in the next morning.

Then I made the mistake of suggesting that he might be a little confused, and a day early, because the *Tattler* came out on Tuesdays and Thursdays. He proceeded to scream at me and blame my wheelchair for my low IQ. Well, at least he wasn't like some other crazy customers, who blamed the fact that I was female for my mental "problems." Then he informed me he was looking for the Darbyville paper, which came out on Mondays. When I told him he had to talk to the Darbyville paper, he lectured me on my stupidity, not knowing that all newspapers are owned by the same massive organization, bent on mental control of the entire country through calculated misinformation. I got ticked enough to tell him to look around the office. Did he see a display rack for the Darbyville paper? That meant if we didn't have it on the premises, then we didn't handle the paper.

I admit, I snarked at him, and told him I wouldn't touch the Darbyville paper with fire tongs. Granted, this was because the Pikes had just played the Darbyville Hounds, and there were four near-fights on the football field. The Hounds got slapped for unsportsmanlike conduct, which just triggered another unsportsmanlike action and another penalty. And so on.

So yeah, I had it in for anything and anyone Darbyville that particular afternoon. I might have sounded a little more than snarky when I made the comment about the fire tongs. That shut him up for maybe three seconds, so chances were it got through to him, at least a little, that he was demanding blood from a stone. Of course, any blink of common sense faded out immediately, because he then insisted that even though we didn't write, print or distribute the newspaper, we had an obligation to him as a resident of Neighborlee. Didn't I know that all newspapers were owned by the local government? That meant I was a government employee and therefore I worked for him, to make sure his newspaper was delivered on time.

I didn't have the energy to argue with his twisted logic and nastiness. I wanted to get him out of the office, or at least make him stand about ten feet away. All his screaming had produced a fine spray of spit that was settling on the front of my sweater. I could see past him out the window of the door, with a good view of his car. He had parked in front of the door, despite the signs that clearly said, "no parking" and "fire truck lane." So, I reached with my mind, using some of the tricks Kurt had taught me over the years about cars, and turned on his horn and windshield wipers and lights. He ran, cursing and tripping over his own feet, to stop his car, and blamed some kids, even though there were no kids visible. He had quite an extensive vocabulary of profanity. While his back was turned, I locked the door and turned off all the lights and waited until he finally got his car under control and peeled out of the parking lot.

So when I saw Cromwell shuffling down the street on that frigid January night, my first inclination was to take a few pictures of him in his weird outfit to post on social media. And share with our circulation department, and the Darbyville paper's circulation department, because they despised him too. Enemy of my enemy is my friend, and all that. Then I realized he was shuffling barefoot through the icy slush and didn't seem to be feeling any pain. Was the guy on drugs? Drunk? His eyes were open, and they almost seemed to be crossed. He wasn't doing the Frankenstein walk, but there was just something about his posture that made me think of all those stereotyped, B-grade zombie movies. Or people walking through the streets, drooling and chanting, "Im. Ho. Tep."

I called the Neighborlee police and reported the sighting. Jasmine Poe was on dispatch duty, and she asked me if I would stay with Cromwell until a cruiser showed up. Anyone else, I might have suspected them of disbelieving me, and trying to keep me in one place, so someone could come arrest me for a false report. This was Jasmine, however, a member of my church. She knew me, she knew where I lived. I agreed, and kept about ten feet behind Cromwell as he continued shuffling down the street, with my headlights firmly focused on him.

At the next intersection, I caught movement out of the corner of my eye and slowed enough to see another sleepwalker heading our way. I called back to report the second walker. This time I talked to Vince Gagliotti, whom we had very unfairly and unkindly called a vampire when we were children. It turned out he had a skin condition that made him photosensitive, so he couldn't go out between dawn and dusk. Night jobs were all he could take, or else wear long sleeves and gloves and hats with really big brims, dark glasses, and sunscreen about an inch thick on his face. Vince was a great guy and very forgiving, and a well-known writer of a middle grade series about -- what else? -- vampire kids. He probably worked as a dispatcher just to have contact with real human beings. He told me that the switchboard had five calls about people looking like Cromwell since I called in. I bit my tongue to keep from retorting that they couldn't have looked as ridiculous as Cromwell.

When the patrol car showed up, Chuck O'Donnell, Clarice's brother, was driving. He asked if I would stay with him and keep an eye on the second sleepwalker, whenever they split off from each other. They weren't really walking together, but the second sleepwalker, a woman I didn't know, was walking almost in Cromwell's steps. Like he had broken the trail for her.

They didn't split up. We got to Overlook, the main drag through town that effectively divided Neighborlee in half. The light was red, but Cromwell and the woman kept walking. And there was a car coming, scattering slush, with a radio booming. From what I could see, the windows were open. My guess? The driver was half-asleep and fighting to stay awake with cold air and noise. I knew I was right, because I was guilty of that tactic a few times. Chuck must have realized at the same time I did, chances were good the oncoming driver wouldn't see Cromwell, who was already halfway across the curb lane, until it was too late. He hit the siren and the brights and pulled out into traffic. I braced for the crash for two seconds before I had a "Well, duh, dummy, do something, you're a superhero!" moment.

I reached with my brain and yanked hard on Cromwell and the woman, pulling them backward hard enough to make them fall with an almost audible splat, and a wide splash of road slush. The oncoming driver swerved wide, going into the opposite lane, hit his horn, and kept going. But I would bet big money his heart was racing and adrenaline kept him awake for the remainder of the drive home.

Cromwell and the woman woke up, confused and shivering ferociously enough to make up for however long they had been walking in the slush. I had a car blanket, and I pulled it out for the woman until the EMTs came in response to Chuck's call. She needed it, since she was wearing nothing but baby doll pajamas and fuzzy pink Hello Kitty knee socks, which were soaked and crusty with ice. Seriously? Baby doll pajamas in February? Chuck had one of those silvery space-age emergency blankets in his cruiser, which he gave Cromwell to wrap up in. Cromwell didn't recognize me, fortunately. And yes, I did snap a few pictures, for the benefit of the circulation managers who had gone through similar arguments with Cromwell.

Heinrich was our police beat reporter, and he gave me all his notes when he pulled together the story Tuesday, scrambling to get it ready to print Wednesday, for the next edition of the *Tattler*. A grand total of sixteen people went sleepwalking in various stages of undress and ridiculous sleepwear that night. Most of them left their houses without closing their doors behind them. There might have been more people, but those were the ones who were spotted by other late-night drivers and patrol cars. All were stopped by one means or another before they crossed against a traffic light or stepped out in front of oncoming traffic that was ignoring stop signs and yield signs because of the lateness of the hour. None of those people, when taken to the hospital and given blood tests, had any drugs or other substances in their systems to explain why they suddenly started sleepwalking when they didn't have any known history of sleepwalking.

After the story ran in the paper, Heinrich got phone calls from people who reported members of their family acting strange, trying to get out of the house, failing because they couldn't operate a lock, or someone stopped them. Other people woke up somewhere in their homes with frozen limbs and wet clothes, signs of having been outside, but no memory of leaving and coming back. Plus there was the frightening moment when people woke up and realized doors outside were hanging open. In some instances, pets escaped outside. In others, inside doors slammed open or closed from a change of air pressure, startling people awake. On a hunch, Heinrich checked with the police and tracked down a sudden rash of reports for the last week of attempted break-ins, all with doors hanging open, but no signs or clues to who had been trying, and no damage to the doors indicating if they had been picked or forced.

So yes, the sleepwalking had been going on for a week now. How could I have been the first one to see a walker? It didn't make sense.

Chief Tanner instituted a patrol, authorizing overtime for officers who spent their nights looking specifically for walkers. He had been around Neighborlee long enough to know that such strange behavior wouldn't be one-and-done. Even if people prepared to deal with the odd behavior, it would keep going.

Well, he was partly right. No sleepwalkers were spotted the Tuesday night after I ran into Cromwell, or Wednesday night, but on Thursday after the story ran, twenty sleepwalkers appeared, all getting out of their beds and leaving their homes within a forty-five-minute window of time. The volunteer officers had been instructed not to wake the sleepwalkers, but they were to try to detour the people and guide them back home. Whenever a patrol car pulled across the street and blocked the way, the sleepwalkers bumped up against the cars, and after a minute or two, turned around and went back the way they came.

Our team was up in the air, flying as low as we could get to spot walkers. We stopped ten people ourselves, between 11pm and 2am. We turned all of them back, either using my telekinesis or Jane setting up a barrier of the Ghost field to block them. Everyone turned back. Then after 2am, the sleepwalkers just stopped appearing.

The next two nights -- nothing. Nobody walking. Then the

third night, Sunday, the walkers showed up again. This time, between the people we turned around and the ones the police reported, there were more than thirty walkers. The police got them to turn back like they had before. We turned back most of the people we spotted, but we were curious to see just how long people would walk if we didn't bounce them directly back the way they had come. We set up barriers at intersections, angled, to guide people down side streets but not turn them completely around and go home.

This time, the sleepwalkers kept appearing and walking until nearly 3am.

Monday, Harry returned from his trip to the Fae Realms. He had no real success, but he had hope that the researchers he had contacted and given information could come up with answers about the odd energy he had detected in the un-compressed tunnel. He joined our patrol. Wednesday night was the third night since the last walkers appeared, firmly establishing a pattern of every third night. This time, eight more sleepwalkers, and an increase of nearly fifty minutes of walking time.

This time, we did our best to identify people, so we could collect names and addresses, and try to find what they had in common to cause the sleepwalking. Portia was with us, and Ford, Athena and Doni, Cosmo and Wallace, Felicity and Jake. Daniel officially assigned me to work with Heinrich, so I had an excuse to question the police officers who were helping with the patrol for walkers. They had been taking down names of people they recognized, and when they could follow walkers all the way home, collecting addresses. The first, easiest pattern to pick up was that the same people were walking, with new faces and names added to the list each time. We shared with Chief Tanner all the information we could from our patrols, and he reciprocated with everything his officer volunteers had been noting. It didn't help much, and we were really hoping that the sleepwalking would stop just as mysteriously as it had started. These late night hours were starting to wear me down, and I didn't look forward to flying patrol in the cold every third night for months to come, thanks very much. To misquote Indiana Jones, it wasn't my age or the late hours, it was the mileage!

That first night he went out with us, Harry felt an energy in the ground, echoed by a faint song in the air he couldn't clearly identify. The kind of frightening aspect of the sleepwalker incidents was that we had finally come up against an energy, a kind of magic, that Kurt and Jane couldn't sense. No, we didn't share that specific bit of information with the Chief. What good would it do? We would waste a lot of time explaining the as-yet inexplicable.

Bethany joined us on our nighttime patrols, walking with Harry and using his invisibility "problem" to let them move around without getting people suspicious. Daniel joined us, and I somehow ended up in his truck instead of flying. We let Kurt and Jane take the aerial patrol, while Felicity and Jake were in his truck, Portia and Ford in his, and the next generation -- meaning Athena, Wallace, Doni and Cosmo -- on foot. We had the town covered the best we could.

We had a warm snap, not unusual for February in Northeast Ohio, so by the fifth night, Saturday, February 5, the walkers were navigating through rain and sleet, but at least no snow in the streets. That was good because many were barefoot. We recorded more than fifty now, walking until just past 5am. Despite the public service announcements trying, discretely, to ask people to watch out for the signs of sleepwalkers, the police were still getting calls from people who woke up, startled to find their clothes and hair and bedding were wet and their feet scraped and muddy.

We tried to turn back as many people as we could, putting our vehicles in the center of the road, to make the walkers rebound and go back the way they came or makeshift roadblocks for those who didn't have vehicles. Doni and Cosmo experimented and came up with a simple tactic. The foot patrol members got two two-by-twos each, about five feet long, easily carried over their shoulders. When they ran into walkers, they just got in front of their target and held the poles out to block them. That was enough obstruction to get the walker turned around and rebounding back home.

Chapter Twelve

We gathered up some disturbing statistics. All the walkers were fairly new residents of Neighborlee. None of them had been born in town. None had been living among us longer than five years. All came from the east side of Neighborlee, with Overlook Drive, the main drag through town, being the dividing line. And apparently the goal for all the walkers. Why they wanted or needed to cross Overlook, we had yet to discover. When we experimented and let people keep walking because there was no traffic to threaten them, they always headed for Overlook. Nearly a straight line. They would have crossed the street if we would let them. We didn't, though. Being the main drag through town, a lot of people used Overlook to get to other towns and highway entrances. Overlook was a thirty-five zone, and once it got dark and rush hour was over, a lot of non-Neighborlee people decided it was okay to raise the speed limit to forty-five, and after midnight there were always people who tried to go fifty. They must have had radar detectors, because they usually managed to slow before they could get caught. Radar detectors wouldn't protect sleepwalkers who got in their way doing fifty. All we needed was one walker trying to cross where the streetlights weren't good, right into the path of an oncoming car, with a driver in too much a hurry to pay attention to what he saw in his headlights.

Sunday night, the guardians met at Divine's.

"Why isn't anyone from the west side of Overlook walking?" Ford said.

"Because ... they already are where they want to be?" Bethany offered, coming into Angela's living/dining room with a pot of tea. She set it on the table and moved aside for Athena, who was carrying the tray of cookies.

"That could be part of it," Portia said. She was curled up on a couch, flipping through the ring binder of the reports we had assembled on all the walkers. "It could be that there are so few people walking on this side of town that none of the patrols have caught them."

"Or something on this side of town stops them from walking." Jane looked up from her phone. "Beau says they're set up to do rapid blood tests, even breath tests, if we can figure out how to get samples without waking up any of the walkers. Demetrius has all the paperwork and fake I.D. cards, to send the survey teams through town, to try to figure out what people have been doing different lately, eating different, maybe sounds and smells that aren't normal."

"Going on three weeks now," Kurt said, "how would they know that something isn't normal? It's become routine."

"True." Portia looked up as Angela came into the room, carrying a second tea pot. "But maybe Jane has the answer. There are three places ..." She shook her head and a grim smile twisted her lips. "Actually, quite a few places on this side of the road that might be resisting whatever is causing people to walk." She put aside the binder and sat up, putting her feet down on the floor, and ticked off each item on her fingers. "Divine's, for starters. Jane's spa, which I can testify is full of unusual energy. And there are the quarries, which we all know are full of interesting substances and odd events. Even if Jinx's pool did get emptied at long last. And our church. Don't underestimate the protective power buildup of prayers over the long term."

"So all our places being on this side of town is ... what?" I said. "Soaking up whatever magic influence or alien mind control rays are making people walk on the other side of the street, so people here are protected?"

"Or those people are more easily influenced on that side of the road," Angela said. She sat down carefully and rested her hands flat on the table, on either side of the tray with the flavored creams and honey and sugar.

"Maybe we should ask what's on the east side of Overlook," Daniel said. "Maybe what's there is causing them to walk, and what's on the east side of the street wants to get at something on the west side of the street, and maybe ..." He shrugged. "Maybe it is sending sleepwalkers because it can't get to this side of the street? Just like it can't make people on this side of the street walk?" Another shrug. An uneasy grin. "Why are all of you looking at me like that?"

"Like what?" I said.

"Like I grew an extra head?"

"How about a bigger brain than the rest of us?" Kurt muttered. "Yeah, something on the east side of ..." He closed his eyes and slumped back in the couch next to Jane. "The flower shop."

"Them again?" Stanzer opened his mouth, and I could almost see in his eyes some snarky remark about Kerri or whoever was inside that dark cloud, without the sense to learn their lesson. Then his eyes widened, and some horrid realization made him pause.

"They keep trying to get to Overlook, and our efforts keep them from crossing the road," Angela said. "What would happen if we let them cross? They want something on this side of the road. If we get an idea what it is, that might also give us an idea who is behind the sleepwalking, and maybe what they want."

Stanzer made a choking sound, and a shiver ran down my back. He knew something, but either he couldn't say it, or he didn't want to say it.

"Maybe we don't want to get that close to them getting it," Ford said. "Ever think that just letting them cross the street will ..." He sighed. "I don't know, break a barrier, let things loose, or maybe let something in that shouldn't get in?"

"How will we know?" Daniel said.

Stanzer snapped off some guttural words that nearly put a smell of sulfur in the air. Definitely curse words from his homeworld or dimension or whatever. Dawn, who was helping Athena and Bethany with the refreshments, flinched and nearly dropped the stack of plates she was carrying.

"What?" Daniel said.

"My office, my building, is on the west side of Overlook," Stanzer said with a quiet tone that was like a shout for its intensity. "Dawn is on the west side. What if they're after her?"

We were all silent. Athena and Bethany moved up closer to Dawn, and got those determined, defensive expressions on their faces that made me so proud of them.

"I hope you are wrong, and yet ..." Angela sighed. "We must consider all possibilities, prepare for the worst, and hope for the best."

We debated theories for another hour, and procedures for dealing with the walkers so they weren't hurt. Chief Tanner had already recommended that the families of all the walkers do their best to keep them home, whatever it took, starting with either keeping the walkers awake, or locking their bedroom doors. We asked Pastor Rocky for volunteers from church to walk the streets and keep track of people who didn't have families to stop them from getting out of the house. The focus would be on turning people back as soon as possible. The important thing was to frustrate the enemy and deny him his goal of getting people across Overlook.

Just how much energy and effort on the enemy's part would it take before he could make people on the west side of Overlook start walking?

Fortunately, many family members of walkers weren't as skeptical as they could have been. While the Neighborlee effect made a lot of people oblivious to the weirdness around them, it also made them a little more willing to believe when something weird and possibly dangerous happened near them. While a number of people slept right through their family members leaving the house and coming back, they couldn't sleep through the wet clothes and doors hanging open and bare feet that were cut and bruised and suffered frostbite for no apparent reason. They did the best they could to keep their family members home and safe, and when they couldn't keep a parent or sibling or child from escaping the house, they got dressed and walked with them, and brought dry clothes and shoes to put on them when or if they ever woke up. And they asked for help. The pressure of the requests for help worked in our favor.

Arthur Sheridan got busy pulling strings and finding help and specialists to deal with the situation from a non-guardian, non-magical level. That Tuesday, a story ran in the *Tattler* as a public service announcement, to keep people aware of the situation and to offer help. All the walkers and their families were sent information packets. A doctor on the Sheridan team was a sleep researcher. He was willing to take anyone who was interested, or desperate, or just plain scared, and give them a preliminary examination. That started with a long survey covering everything they had been eating, where they had been going over the last month, any unusual events, any strange dreams, on and on. Part of the help included those blood tests and exams the gang at Hoax wanted to conduct, but couldn't without waking up the sleepwalkers. If an enemy was controlling the walkers, we didn't want to risk waking them, unless the situation was dire. Like they were determined to step out into traffic.

That night, the only people who got out of their houses without someone noticing were people who lived alone. Maybe ten people. That was a victory, and yet created a new problem for us. Finding and tracking ten people was a lot harder than we anticipated, because we were still trying to cover a huge area. After all, we didn't dare work on the assumption that the walking was only happening on the east side of Overlook. There could be walkers on the west side, just very few, on streets without lights, falling into the shadows, so to speak, and being missed by the patrols.

One of the ten we did find walking got within five sidewalk squares of Overlook Drive, before Kurt and Jane saw him and swooped down and stopped him. A little nerve-wracking. What was the balance between wearing ourselves out looking for decreased numbers, to keep them out of trouble, and waiting for the numbers to grow large enough that they were easier to track?

We considered just letting people walk and focus on patrolling all the streets that touched Overlook Drive, to keep them from crossing. Yet if we could intervene and send people home before they got drenched or frozen or hurt their bare feet, didn't we have a responsibility to do so?

The information lines the police department had set up filed reports of family members trying to leave the house in the middle of the night and waking everyone else in the house, including dogs and cats and pet birds. New people were added to the list of those being roused from bed to sleepwalk. What did our enemy want? How much energy did he or they have to spend on this effort to get people across the street?

Then a new problem appeared, coming from outside of Neighborlee. Whether it was another tactic of the enemy, or just the increasing nastiness level in general of our society, we couldn't determine, and quite frankly didn't have the time to analyze. Outsiders knew about our problem, and they were taking advantage of it, for their own amusement and profit.

First, it was just the information line getting an increasing number of crank calls, outsiders who thought the stories of sleepwalkers was funny and were trying to make trouble or just skew the numbers. Then on the next walking night, Friday the 11th, Kurt and Jane stopped a half-dozen people who were driving around town with their lights off, looking for sleepwalkers. The police officially stopped news crews from four different TV and radio stations, driving up and down residential streets, looking for walkers. They didn't appreciate being told that what they were doing was violating the privacy of the victims. Monday, Valentine's Day, City Council members got calls from several university research departments, wanting to do a study of the air and water of Neighborlee. Local stations dredged up the whole New Year's Eve mess from two years ago, when Sylvia Grandstone died, and there was all that talk about toxic fumes coming up from underground.

Yeah, I know I was hoping for something to distract all of us, especially Daniel, and take the emphasis off Valentine's Day, but I cannot take all the blame for the weirdness quotient rising so fast and furiously. And yes, the expected deluge of Valentine's Day losers, asking for either absolution or advice from Terry when they messed up on the big romance day of the year, decreased noticeably from previous years, but I certainly didn't get to enjoy it.

The important thing was that nobody got near Overlook Drive. We didn't have any new walkers on Monday night.

Harry and Lori asked some friends from a handful of Fae academic institutions to study the air and soil and plants and the energy fields. At least, they said those people were supposed to come. If they found anything, they didn't tell Harry and Lori. If they showed up at all, Harry and Lori didn't know. Angela just smiled faintly and rolled her eyes when I grumbled about the lack of communication.

Then on Wednesday, the enemy finally got frustrated to the point of bringing out the big guns: the doppelganger.

We had been encouraging the guardians and our allies among the Sheridan people to stay within the borders of Neighborlee as much as possible, to the point of canceling appointments and activities. That was easier for some people, but not for others, like Daniel, who had his office in Independence. We were still thinking of tactics for keeping people on the alert to the problem of evil twins showing up without turning it into a big mess. I didn't really mind canceling two comedy gigs, especially after my evil twin showed up at the comedy club and made things weird with the people who knew me there. My mistake was in thinking that public venues and publicized activities were my only vulnerable points.

I had a speaking commitment at a career day event for the Darbyville schools. It was being held at the Darbyville community center, for middle school age upwards. The organizer, Vanessa, was something of a friend, so I couldn't say no without looking like a selfish louse. This was a win-win for her because I could talk about teaching and coaching and journalism and comedy and dealing with a physical handicap, and she could save money on the honorarium fees for four other speakers. It was good PR for the *Tattler*, too. I didn't think about canceling, because again, I didn't want to look or feel like a louse. Plus, I didn't think anyone but Vanessa's team knew I was coming. It wasn't like they were going to advertise the event and invite other school districts to participate, right? It wasn't like the doppelganger could follow me from Neighborlee, less than a quarter mile over the border to the community center, which was attached to the city hall and police and fire departments.

The unfair part in all this? I didn't even say something stupid, like "What could happen?"

My first clue that something strange was going on was when I rolled up to the information desk to sign in and find out what room I was assigned to. I knew Pam, the woman at the desk, the nerve center for the day's events. She gave me an odd look and took a half-step back.

"What happened?" she asked, leaning forward again and lowering her voice, like she didn't want anyone to hear her asking.

"To what?"

"You're back in your chair."

"Back? But I just got here."

That got more wrinkles around her eyes and mouth, and that tendency to lean away from me. Like maybe she thought I was crazy. Or dangerous.

Then I caught on and caught up.

"Oh ... heck. Pam, did someone who looks like me show up a little while ago?"

No way could I say "my evil twin" or "doppelganger." That would just make things weirder than they already were. And increasing exponentially with every word we said to each other.

"There's some wacko who's trying to make trouble for me with the comedy clubs where I've been performing. Trying to steal my career or ruin it or whatever. I don't know what her problem is with me, but … she's not in a wheelchair, is she?"

Pam just shook her head, but her hunched shoulders visibly relaxed.

"The comedy clubs have been warned and they're locking her out, so now I guess she's coming after me other places. Where did she go? I'll take care of it, no problem. Better tell Vanessa, but tell her I'll take care of it quietly. I hope."

Pam pointed and I thanked her and spun my wheelchair around to head down the long hallway of meeting rooms. I ducked into the first one and got my phone out. While I waited for Kurt to pick up, I pivoted around to sit in the doorway and look down the hall for my evil twin. What were the chances I could just throw all my brain power into making my chair go sub-light speed and run her over, turn her into a grease smear on the tile floor, and end the problem in a highly satisfying and messy fashion?

Probably not that good.

"Hey," I said when Kurt picked up. "I'm in Darbyville and my evil twin is here. Any chance --"

"We'll be there in maybe twenty minutes, max." Then he hung up.

So very not good. He didn't know where I was in Darbyville, did he?

No, Kurt didn't know. I got hold of London and asked her to alert everybody to what was happening. We were talking about her accessing the security cameras throughout the building when Kurt called back. London laughed. I had told her, after all, that Kurt hung up without getting that crucial information from me. She promised to get back to me when she had something and blanked the screen.

"I'm in the west wing of the community center," I told him, without giving him a chance to even say hi. "It's career day for the school kids. My first talk is supposed to start in half an hour. Any chance we can clear this up without having any inconvenient witnesses?"

"Doubt it."

"London's searching the security system to locate her."

"Good. We're on our way." He hung up again, and I swear I heard a whisper of Jane's laughter somewhere in the background.

Daniel called me next. And scared me into nearly leaping out of my chair, because he laughed at the new ringtone I had assigned to his number *before* I answered the phone.

It was the Darth Vader theme by John Williams, from *Star Wars*, and he was five steps down the hall from me.

"Just got the alert from London," he said, stepping into the doorway and grabbing one handle of my chair to pull it back further into the room.

I was so startled, I let him.

"What are you doing here?"

"Checking up on a valued employee making a public appearance and being the face of the corporation." His smile was flat, and that was worry, not humor glinting in his eyes. "I know it's a dumb question, now, but do you realize what danger you just rolled into?"

"I do now, thanks."

"That woman at the information desk needs to cut down on the caffeine. I asked where you were, and she said, 'which one?' That was the first clue. When I said I wanted the one in a wheelchair, she pointed me this way, and then I got the alert from London." He closed his eyes and rubbed the bridge of his nose. "Kind of handy, having her and Sherwood helping out."

"Yeah, but what are we going to do about my evil twin? How do we explain two of us, besides saying I've got a wacko stalker trying to ruin my career and my reputation?"

"That sounds like a good start."

Amazingly, we were able to laugh a little bit.

We knew the situation was too serious to hide in the unused meeting room, making snarky comments. We headed down the hall. Daniel walked next to me instead of behind my chair. I had the awful feeling he was going to depend on his invulnerability gift and throw himself in front of me if the doppelganger attacked.

As it turned out, I didn't have to deal with my evil twin. She must have either seen me coming, or had heard someone say I had showed up, or the word was getting around about a lookalike on the premises. The next thing I knew, Dawn was running down the hallway to me, her face pale and her eyes full of tears.

"Miss Zephyr, you have got to help me! I am in so much trouble!" she wailed.

First clue this wasn't Dawn Dover? The real Dawn never called me Miss Zephyr. I was Lanie from the day she moved to Neighborlee.

Second clue: her clothes and her voice. Dawn preferred jeans and flat shoes, either sneakers or sandals. This Dawn was in sleek style with two-inch heels on strappy sandals -- in February? -- and a bright red, long sweater coat that hung to her calves, over a spaghetti-strap black top and matching black pants. She also had these chandelier-style earrings that tinkled when she moved, and glossy purplish lipstick and smoky eye makeup. Definitely not Dawn Dover. Because hey, third clue: she should have been in school, in Neighborlee. Dawn wasn't the kind of kid who skipped classes.

I cataloged all those wrong details later. All I knew in that moment was that the Dawn I knew wouldn't dress like that. And Dawn wasn't the type to wail. Or whine. Or whimper.

"Please, you have to take me home right now. I am in so much trouble!" She reached out, probably to grab hold of my arm.

Daniel stepped in front of me. I nearly yelled for him to get out of the way and not let her touch him. Well, duh, that was what he was trying to prevent happening to me. I didn't trust that immunity talent of his. There was always a first time for our weird gifts to fail, right? I was living proof of that.

Yet how could I *know* that the fake Dawn touching either of us would do any damage? Maybe let the doppelganger suck all the salt from my blood, like in Star Trek's *Mantrap* episode? Or inject acid into my blood to erase me? Or drugs to take over my mind and make me its slave?

"Sure, why not?" I grabbed my wheels and turned around so sharply I nearly threw myself out of my chair.

It was good I moved that fast, because the fake Dawn sidestepped Daniel and was still reaching for me. She missed, going to her knees on the floor where I used to be. I swear I saw sparks dancing on her fingertips.

Nope, definitely did not want to let her touch me.

Chapter Thirteen

More sparks danced along the doorknobs up and down the hall. Felicity stepped out of thin air, which naturally meant she had hitched a ride with Jane or Jane and Kurt, and they were right behind her, still invisible in the Ghost field.

Whew!

Felicity glared and spread her arms and sparks burst from her fingertips. I raised my hands to let go of the chrome on my chair, even though Felicity had enough fine control now, she would never zap me. No matter how distracted she got.

At least, I hoped so.

The lights in the ceiling flared almost painfully bright, then died. That hallway was dark. The only light came from the lobby behind us.

The fake Dawn glowed, like swamp gas, as she struggled to get to her feet.

"But Miss Zephyr, you don't understand!"

Seriously? Couldn't this idiot tell the gig was up? The game was over?

Umm, yeah, someone or something so sloppy or in a hurry that she couldn't get details right when she impersonated someone probably *was* that stupid. Or at least that oblivious.

Would that work in our favor?

She reached for me again, while I was analyzing. If my swirling thoughts could be charitably called analyzing.

"No you don't," Jane snarled from behind me.

The Ghost field flickered into life between me and the doppelganger.

She let out a wail as the Ghost field enclosed her and she vanished, cutting off whatever she was going to say.

Okay, that was good timing. Jane had just saved my bacon, but what were we supposed to do?

"We've got her," Kurt said, stepping out of the Ghost field. "Not sure how long we can keep her. Let's head for the border and get this over with, maybe get some answers." Then he vanished before I could do more than nod, and ask some really important questions, such as where exactly we were going.

Daniel grabbed my wheelchair handles and Felicity ran ahead of us. He was thinking much faster than me right then, and came up with a plan before we got to the information desk and Pam.

"Look sick, and let me do the talking," he said.

Right then, I realized that the encounter had drained me, because I didn't get angry, I didn't question him. I found it far too easy to slump in my wheelchair. Felicity later told me I did look pale and my hands were shaking a little. I prefer to think that was from fury. Daniel told Pam the imposter problem had been dealt with, but she had attacked me. We had to follow the authorities who had taken her out the back way, and deal with her right away. I noticed he didn't say which "back way" had been used, and he didn't say which authorities. Pam likely knew all the back doors and maintenance entrances, and she probably figured the Darbyville cops were involved. Actually, Daniel hadn't said a single lie, he just let Pam make assumptions.

We got outside just as the reinforcements were showing up. Ford pulled up next to the curb, with Bethany, Harry and Angela in the car following him. There were other cars behind them. I wanted to make a smart-alec remark about overkill, but I held back. I had the awful feeling it would come out very lame.

My phone rang while I was pulling myself into the front seat of Daniel's truck. Felicity took my keys and said she would drive my Jeep and meet us. I was too busy to fight her, getting my phone and trying to catch up with what Daniel was telling Ford and others who were gathering around. The call was Kurt. He and Jane were keeping the doppelganger in a separate Ghost field because they didn't trust it not to turn and bite them if they kept it inside the same sphere with them. Smart. They were going to wait for us just a couple blocks away, on a half-deserted residential street, right on the border of Neighborlee and Darbyville. Just in case we all needed to leap over the border and out of the reach of their prisoner, who was snarling and spitting and not exactly looking completely human anymore. So could we hurry?

I didn't connect the address until Daniel and I were leading a caravan out of the municipal lot, up a gravel road that was an unofficial shortcut and undedicated street, and into a half-built residential section. This area was right on the edge of the Metroparks, close to where the Rivals had ambushed Hayward two Christmases ago, and the place where Athena and Doni had run afoul of that idiot rookie Darbyville cop.

Even more important, it was one street away from that house where something had taken up residence and tried to take a bite out of Angela, during that social experiment my freshman year of college.

"I don't know, Han," I murmured, trying to joke away the twisting, dropping sensation in my stomach. "I'm getting a bad feeling about this."

Daniel gave me a concerned look. Unfortunately, we didn't have enough time for me to explain the context before we were turning down the street. It was paved, but only had six houses, all at the far end where it met another street. Most of the lots were just marked by stakes to indicate where the sidewalk would go, and those green tubes that protected the hookups for gas and water and sewer lines. From the mud and faded colors of the flags on the stakes, nothing had been built here in years. I had to wonder what had happened. Maybe there was some kind of blight touching this street, and the ones adjacent to it, thanks to the nasty magic or alien power fields that had touched that house on the next street. I wondered if anyone had ever bought that house, or if it still sat there with a shaggy lawn, and blight creeping into the neighbors' lawns.

Daniel drove slowly down the street until we got to the line where Neighborlee started and the malign influence on Darbyville stopped. The lots were still empty, but the mud wasn't churned up in ruts, and gravel marked where driveways would be. The grass and bushes and saplings looked healthy, almost cheerful. That was saying a lot, since this was February in Ohio.

"In case we need to run fast, park up there," I said, and pointed at the green.

Daniel didn't question, just paused to look it over, and I could see him making the connection between the brown of dead grass and mud, and the early spring burst of life, a clear dividing line. Bethany, Harry and Angela pulled up next to us. I was sure Angela had seen the safe zone, but I did not want her there. I imagine she didn't really want to be there, so close to the place where something nasty had tried to drain her. Ford and Charlotte were next.

Kurt and Jane stepped out into visibility once the rest of the gang had turned onto the street. He made sure everyone parked on the Neighborlee side of the street. Jane was busy, arms spread and hands kind of curled up into claws, her eyes half-closed in concentration. I imagined she was having a bit of a struggle keeping the doppelganger prisoner. What did it look like, hidden inside the Ghost field? Kurt had said "not quite human."

"Uh, Angela, maybe you should stand back?" Kurt said, when Jane lowered her arms and a hazy, swirling globe of gray mist appeared out of thin air. It was maybe about ten feet in diameter and pulsed in a few spots, so it wasn't exactly a perfect sphere.

A *buzz-snap-crack* sound startled all of us. Even Jane flinched. The mist had been a dirty white until then, but now darkened and cracks of poison-green light crazed the surface.

"Indeed, not," Angela said quietly. She stood up straight and pulled her shoulders back and walked slowly toward the sphere, which was rotating kind of crazy. I imagined a rabid hamster inside, its fur multiple colors, shooting off sparks, and racing inside its wheel fast enough to generate electricity. "What are you, creature? Speak, and reveal your master and your mission." Her voice had a hollow tone to it, like she spoke from far away, and a distant time, in a massive place.

I swear, if a raspy voice, kind of like Gozer from the *Ghostbusters* movie, had answered, I would have totally regained my flying ability, getting out of there fast enough to create a sonic boom.

The crazing of the globe shattered and this ugly kind of dust or snow swirled around inside the globe. The fake Dawn didn't look anything remotely like her anymore. It bounced off the sides, snarling and spitting and kind of hairy, dressed in ragged clothes that looked like every color, underneath the impression of filth. It slowed and swirled around to hang there in mid-air, its whole body heaving with deep breaths. It glared at Angela, and drool dripped from one side of its mouth. Then it smiled, baring sharp teeth.

It lunged at Angela.

It hit the Ghost field.

Jane shrieked. The field shattered, hitting her with a burst of pale, ugly green light. The color of bad guacamole just before it bursts into mold in the back of the refrigerator. She fell backward.

The doppelganger flew, straight at Angela.

She just stood there, calm, with this odd, crooked little smile, like she was expecting it.

At the last moment, Angela raised her arms, blocking the doppelganger that I swear was opening its jaws three times wider than it should have, and aiming for her throat. It caught hold of her wrists.

Angela turned with utter grace, seeming to move in slow motion, and with a sweep of her arms she flung the doppelganger away.

All this in the space of maybe three heartbeats.

Fury and terror took over. I leaped from my chair and threw myself at Angela with everything I had, and we both flew back ten feet, into the green, wet grass on the Neighborlee side.

Howling and spitting and snarling, the doppelganger flew at us, almost like a mirror image of what I had done.

It hit the dividing line of Neighborlee and Darbyville, and for two seconds, the shield became visible. It lit up like a demonic Christmas tree, appropriate for a *Walking Dead* Christmas special. The doppelganger howled and flew backward, smoking and writhing.

I was furious. I leaped after it. I caught it.

The biggest gong in all of creation went off in my head and vibrated through my bones and I found myself on the ground, gasping for breath, and suddenly seasick because the planet was undulating underneath me.

"It's caught hold of her," Angela shouted. "Bring her to me."

She stood on the Neighborlee side, holding out her arms, and I felt even more sick seeing that flicker of panic on her face. Angela never panicked about anything. Was that my fault?

Daniel and Kurt caught hold of me under my arms and lifted. They hurried the dozen or so feet to get me to the green grass and safety inside Neighborlee's borders, while that *thing* struggled to get to its feet, snarling, its features warping to look like me, but skeletal and furry, and getting more boney and furry with every heartbeat. They took four steps, carrying me, then suddenly something tightened around me and nearly yanked me out of their arms. They stopped with a jolt, almost pulled off their feet.

Thin, ugly, dark lines like hundreds of threads spun through the air between me and the doppelganger. My body burned like molten needles piercing in all those contact points. Daniel and Kurt grunted and lunged forward, dragging me back. The threads dug in deeper into my skin. Thousands of tiny, poison-hot hooks threatened to pull my skin off my flesh.

The burning turned to tingling. Okay, that was ...

No, that wasn't an improvement. The tingling faded to numbness.

"Hurry," I groaned. That sense of nothingness that had terrified me into runny-nose tears and terror in the hospital, right after the night in the quarry ... was returning.

Harry and Jake joined them, grabbing my legs, and they threw themselves forward -- forward for them, backward for me.

"She's catching up," I shouted.

Or tried to. My mouth was going numb and what came out was garbled. Or maybe my ears weren't working right anymore.

Fire washed over my skin, starting with my scalp and racing down my face, squeezing my throat, erupting in my lungs. I screamed, but half of that was relief as well as pain, because I could *feel* again.

The guys fell, going to their knees in the damp, green, Neighborlee-blessed grass. I opened my eyes in time to see the doppelganger hurtling toward us, maybe pulled by those same threads that had been draining me of life. It slammed into the shield again, this time erupting into flames and a writhing cloud of black and poisonous red and green smoke.

I passed out. That made sense. Only for a few seconds. I was still half-buried by my rescuers when I caught my breath and opened my eyes.

Mum and Pop caught up with us about then. Dang -- they had called my folks to come help face down my evil twin? What genius made that moronic decision?

I found out later my parents were at Divine's when Angela got the call. Still, I was furious at the risk they took.

The family farmhouse was closer than any other place to take me, such as my own house, or Divine's, so that was where the entire gang went, after heaving me into the back of the cab of Daniel's truck. Mum made me lie down, as much as I was able to stretch out in that space, with my head on her lap. Yeah, sometimes I really do enjoy being a little kid again and cuddled by my mommy. She kept making me open my eyes so she could study them and checking my pulse in my neck and my wrist. Not very encouraging. I felt … well, not fine, not normal, but I felt pretty good for someone who had nearly been sucked dry or empty or whatever by her evil twin from another dimension.

I really hoped the doppelganger was dead. And I have to say, I haven't often felt that way about anyone who really hacked me off or threatened me. Not even Sylvia Grandstone.

When we got to the farmhouse, I insisted on proving that I was feeling fine by walking from Daniel's truck to the back door. Two seconds later, I proved I was a long way away from fine by going to my knees. My legs weren't tingling, they felt more normal than they had felt in years, but they weren't cooperating. I couldn't even lift myself with telekinesis to get up to the railing and pull myself up the steps to the back door.

We all settled in the kitchen, where that huge farmhouse table came in handy. Those who couldn't settle at the table brought chairs in from elsewhere in the house. Mum got a big pot of Angela's special recipe restorative tea going, and we discussed what had happened. After Mum insisted on checking me again. She and Angela shared those concerned looks that made me feel like a little kid again -- meaning they were using those adults-only looks that adults mistakenly think kids can't see and partially interpret and get really frustrated seeing. They were worried about me. Like, duh!

Athena and her gang arrived last. They had examined the site of the battle and near-draining, helping London and Sherwood do some scanning and reading of energy flows. The AI's had taken a dozen or so measuring apps, including some new, not-yet-released apps for businesses like the power companies, and adapted them to try to get readings on the shield. The verdict was that there had been a huge fluctuation in the shield, and a big power drain.

I repeat -- duh!

Right now, the shield was rippling, and the fluctuations were spreading through the air and soil of Neighborlee. Something had destabilized. Through Angela, and through me, power had been drained.

London and Sherwood needed to do more measurements and compare records, but they were afraid we had regressed at least a year in the buildup of power and healing of energy levels in Neighborlee.

Nobody said it, but I could see it in their faces. I refused to say it, because I knew the power of words, and if I spoke what I was thinking ... that would make it real. I had lost a lot of the ground I had gained over the last two years since defeating the Rivals. The healing of my legs, the chance to someday be free of my wheelchair, had reversed.

I put that whining aside for later, when I could be alone and not feel guilty if I indulged in a dark chocolate gorge of self-pity, to drown my sorrows. We had more important things to deal with.

What had been the doppelganger's plan? Had it shown up pretending to be me to cause trouble, or force a confrontation? Why had it chosen to masquerade as Dawn? Why did it want me to take it into Neighborlee? Did it hope I would show it where Dawn lived, and help it pinpoint the source of the energy that attracted it? If I had let it touch me in the community center, would it have drained me then, or just tried to control me? How much damage had I done, how much had I made myself vulnerable, when I tackled it to get it away from Angela? How much had she risked, touching the doppelganger to throw it away? Had we been protected by being close to and then inside Neighborlee's borders? What did the doppelganger want with Angela? Was she the ultimate target, and I was just a convenient means to get to her? It sure seemed to recognize her and go slightly bonkers when it saw her. Like it knew what she was, what she represented, and the power in her grasp. Essentially the keys to the kingdom.

"We need to be ready for another attack," Ford said, after we had talked and even drew some maps and went over the results again with London and Sherwood. "We can't depend on the old pattern when we were dealing with Big Ugly. When we knew we had reprieves between attacks."

"You mean when we thought the defensive shield and the energy were steady?" Angela said, her voice a little quieter than I liked to hear. "When we were sure the enemy had been weakened and needed time to regroup and regain its strength, and come up with a different tactic? This isn't the same enemy. This could be an enemy with many faces."

"Many drones, many soldiers, you mean?" Pop said. "It's a theme showing up in a lot of movies lately, where the foot soldiers are considered expendable, and they're used up to weaken the defenses or tear them down, depending on the genre of movie. So what if you kill off a couple hundred of your soldiers if you've got ten times as many to come flooding in as soon as there's a crack or a pinhole?"

That made too much, depressing sense. So we were ready for the next big strike by the enemy. Or something subtle. In all honesty, we hoped it was something kind of big and flashy, because we didn't want to miss it and have it sneak up on us. Or worse, sneak around us.

~~~~~

The doppelganger accomplished something in that encounter, with me and with Angela. Physical contact had done more than drain power from the shield.

The sleepwalkers went walking again that night, breaking the pattern of every third day, and this time they walked on the west side of Overlook Drive.

Everybody wasted time on patrol, checking with all the people who had been walking over the last few weeks, and nothing happened. I say "everybody" instead of "we" because I wasn't allowed to go out on patrol. Mum and Pop and I went to spend the evening with Angela, because even though she didn't get her circuits zapped like I had, Mum insisted on having both of us together so she could watch over us.

One theory was that since we had both been targets of the doppelganger, and we were together, we triggered the change in the sleepwalkers that night. Like we set off a homing signal. Maybe that had been the goal all along for the encounter at the Darbyville community center: to create a bridge. Maybe if I had let the fake Dawn touch me, if I had taken her into Neighborlee, the enemy would have gotten just what it needed and the next attack would have struck without warning. As it was, the enemy had a better idea of where to send its probes or drones or whatever the sleepwalkers were meant to be.

No matter what we had done wrong that day, no matter what
~~~~~

the doppelganger's goal had been, the damage had been done. Some barrier to the power or influence of the enemy had been broken. Sleepwalkers appeared on the west side of Overlook Drive. Just as we had feared, that was the goal.

With all the focus on looking for walkers on the east side of Overlook, nobody knew they were on the west side, Divine's side of town, for the first half hour, maybe a little less. London and Sherwood registered fluctuations, "pings" of thin streamers of energy being flung at the shield, like darts. Those pings had never happened before. Later they theorized that until that night, the enemy had been using a different level of energy or frequency of mind-control broadcast for the people on the east side of Overlook. Getting past the defenses of Overlook to the west side people, getting through the defensive energy generated by Divine's and Jane's spa and the quarries took a level of energy that got attention, and clashed with the shield.

London and Sherwood strengthened the shield, but with so many of those energy darts being flung, there was too much distraction or irritation to keep track. The hits wore down a weak spot. The energy darts hit that weak spot until they penetrated. Every hit after that expanded the hole. Even when our AI's detected the penetration point, their efforts focused on keeping the hole from growing, rather than shrinking it.

The first dart to hit the ground set up a chain reaction. Kind of like a pebble hitting the water and sending out ripples. London and Sherwood detected those ripples, sent the address of the hit to whoever was closest, and asked them to check it out. By the time Athena and Wallace decided their assigned sleepwalkers weren't walking and got to that side of town, five more darts of enemy energy had repeated the process. Those darts never hit ground in the same spot but spread out.

Wallace was driving, and Athena was in contact with London, and as soon as three darts hit different targets, she started her own search, comparing the addresses with some background research she and Wallace had done.

"We've got trouble," she said, when she called me.

We were sitting around Angela's table, drinking tea and trying to play dominos, because none of us were in the mood to even try to sleep. She called my phone and I put it on speaker.

"As in?" Pop said.

"Those six addresses are all people who are either newcomers to Neighborlee, or most of the members of the family weren't born here."

"Walker spotted," Wallace said, his voice loud. Probably to make sure we could hear him. "Call me paranoid, but if this guy is intending to walk a straight line, I think he's aimed at Divine's."

"Not paranoid at all," Angela said. "It makes frightening sense. This shop has been the target of many attacks all these years."

"It got your scent this afternoon, so now it knows where to aim," I said, catching on to what she had to be thinking.

"Recall everybody," Pop said, raising his voice so Athena could hear him, and probably Wallace too. "Have them get over to this side of town. Prepare for a replay of this afternoon's tactics."

"Circle the wagons?" Mum said.

We called the police department to let them know the walkers were on that side of town now. Then we just sat at the windows and looked out on the quiet, moonlit street, and waited for the puppets of the enemy to show up.

They moved slowly, and those who stayed back for a while to watch the walkers reported that they walked kind of jerky, in tiny steps, like they were walking through high snow. They leaned forward, like walking against a stiff wind.

Fortunately, we didn't rely on our assumption that Angela and Divine's, and probably me, since I had also given the doppelganger a "taste" of me with physical contact, were the targets. The mobile team spread throughout the west side of town, looking for signs of activity, following the blips of the darts of energy through the weak spot in the shield, to see where they landed and who had been awakened to walk.

Some of those walkers weren't headed on a relatively straight line for Divine's. Doni and Cosmo were watching a knot of five walkers and called in regular reports on how they were responding to their surroundings. Meaning when their course took them off a sidewalk into muddy grass, they adjusted to either get back onto the sidewalk or shifted over to walk in the street. At an intersection, when they expected a large turn in the group, to adjust course to head more directly to Divine's, the walkers stayed walking north.

Doni realized they were heading for Stanzer's building when

the walkers crossed another intersection and were now clearly heading away from Divine's. She called in to report it.

Of course. Why would we assume that just because they had homing signals attached to Angela and to me that they had given up trying to get to Dawn? They were on the correct side of the street now, and whatever drew them to Dawn, they were getting the signal loud and clear.

"You sit still," Pop said, leveling a concerned frown at me, just as I was opening up my mouth to say we had to go get Dawn.

Stanzer was out of town, following up on a lead on the origins of Pi Surprise. I had to wonder now if that timing was a little convenient, getting him away from Dawn and taking away some of her defenses. Yes, Gina was staying with Dawn while Stanzer was out of town, so she wasn't alone in the building. The Hounds would show up if she needed them, but it was always smart to avoid needing their intervention. I called Dawn to let her know what we had discovered as Pop ran out the door to get in the van. Angela signaled me to give her the phone, after I told Dawn Pop was on his way, and she and Gina should be ready to head over to join us.

"Pack up whatever you need for a few days," she said. "We should have thought of this, or at least anticipated a breach in our defenses. You're staying with me until this problem is resolved."

"If it's ever resolved," I muttered, when she gave me my phone back.

"There's also the consideration that putting all their targets in one place will just help them focus better," Mum offered. That got an exasperated roll of the eyes from Angela, when my comment didn't even get a flicker of her trademark smirk.

Chapter Fourteen

Within half an hour, Dawn was with us, Divine's had "budded" an extra bedroom for her to use, and Angela decided to take a break from her post at the window to make sandwiches to feed our mobile teams. Pop was disappointed to report that he didn't see a single Hound. Dawn had summoned them to tell them what was happening, so they would let Pop into the building, but they had left before he showed up. Stanzer had managed to communicate to them that no one was allowed into or out of the building at night while he was gone. That had resulted in doors locking and frustrating Gina, when she had tried to step out for an errand just two doors down the street. Dawn hadn't been able to explain what was going on, despite Gina's growing sensitivity to the weirdness factor. She had still argued, despite how weird things were growing, when Pop told her it would be better if she went home. Gina didn't need to go through the mega-dose of Neighborlee weirdness that was about to go down.

The walking started around 1am, calculated from the moment that first dart of enemy power got through the shield. The closest walker was down by the Cutterville border, in the residential area nearest to the flower shop. That kind of made sense, since the closer to the border, the weaker the defensive energy in town. Divine's was the center, the wellspring of the energy we used to defend ourselves and heal ourselves -- and the center of the energy that Big Ugly had been trying to syphon away for decades.

The distance from that area where the first sleepwalkers started out to Divine's would take maybe three-quarters of an hour to walk at a business-like pace in good weather. This was mid-February, and the weather fluctuated constantly, balmy and bright one day, overcast and gusting winds the next, snow for two days, then rain that washed it all away and turned everything to mud. The day had started out mild, but got colder so that puddles had become skating rinks, and even careful steps could turn into involuntary acrobatic exercises. How would these people fare who left their homes barefoot or maybe in socks, and not watching where they were going?

After an hour of monitoring, and finding the other sleepwalkers, we clocked their pace and determined that if Wallace's instincts were right, the sleepwalkers would get to Divine's dead-end street some time after 5am, give or take twenty minutes. There was no traffic speeding through town to threaten the sleepwalkers. They avoided the business district and the municipal zone, so all the streets were residential. That made a difference for those monitoring the walkers and for the walkers themselves.

We had to repeat our assessments multiple times, to get the data from the teams on the road and on foot and flying over the streets, because I had never figured out how to have a conference call on my cell phone. Finally, we agreed to just let the sleepwalkers come. No experimenting with blocking their paths and seeing if they would turn around and go home, or if we could deflect them in another direction and see how soon they corrected course. Kurt and Jane teamed up with Bethany and Harry to swoop around and get pictures of all the walkers, then sent the photos to Chief Tanner. Yeah, he was on duty. As soon as Ford made the call to the police station to report we had walkers on the west side of Overlook, the dispatcher called the Chief. He had left instructions that if anything changed in any way with the sleepwalker situation, he wanted to be notified. He got his people to work, investigating the backgrounds of the walkers, finding out who was at home who might be worried or cause problems when this whole bizarre incident came to its conclusion. Whatever that might have been, whatever the enemy had planned.

With every block closer to Divine's, the walkers slowed. Their feet dragged. There were flickers of distress on their otherwise blank, zombified expressions. Every time a new walker changed direction to join the mass migration heading for Divine's, the teams in their cars and trucks or flying overhead called it in to us. As the stream of people -- we were up to thirty-two by 4:30am -- thickened and the walkers got off the side streets and merged into the same route, they slowed more. Maybe the enemy didn't have as much power to call and control walkers on the west side as they did on the east side of Overlook? So the victims were able to fight whatever was forcing them to walk? Maybe the longer the migration took, the more effort it took? Our favorite theory was that the closer the sleepwalkers got to Divine's, the more the defensive magic built into the walls and foundation interfered with the enemy's control.

"Best case scenario, they stop just short of the final turn," Pop said, making another mark on the rough map we had put together on the dining room table.

We had put all the leaves into the table to extend it as far as it would go. Angela had covered it with a white vinyl tablecloth and dug up a bunch of grease pencils in multiple colors. We kept track of where people had come from on that side of town, how far they had come or still had to go, the time when people joined the main stream of the migration, and Pop even had a calculation for figuring out how much more they would slow down with every intersection they passed.

Once all the walkers who had been found were on the main street, making their shuffling, slow, foot-dragging way toward Divine's, the mobile teams took the long way around them and hurried to Divine's. We settled in at our posts at all the windows, watching them come. It was a little creepy, because a light touch of fog seeped through the night, swirling around the bases of the streetlight poles, but never rising more than three or four feet, so the light spilling down on the fog sort of lay across it. The fog didn't move much as the sleepwalkers walked through it, according to Kurt and Jane, who continued their aerial recognizance. I wanted to be out there, flying and covering a different angle, but Mum and Pop got very stern when I suggested it. They were right, of course. My legs tingled and spasmed at unpredictable moments ever since I was the rope in tug-of-war that morning. I had no assurance of getting airborne, much less staying aloft.

I had a couple new scores to settle with Kerri.

Divine's faced west on the east side of the street, with the hill it sat on sloping north into the Metroparks, and the dead-end street going north-south. I sat at a window in Angela's living room/dining room, looking south, and watching the walkers approaching. A faint silverish glow to my left, which was east, caught my attention. Dawn approached. The leading edge of the sleepwalkers were about five driveways away from the intersection. Our newest calculations had called it pretty close to when they would get to Divine's. Just past 6:45am. I called back to Pop, who was adding new figures to the calculations on the vinyl sheet, to congratulate him that his math was pretty good.

Lights flashed, and for a second there, I thought something was exploding, we just hadn't gotten hit with the sonic boom. Then I realized that was a patrol car with the lights flashing but no siren. It turned down the street, heading for Divine's. It stopped about halfway down the street and turned sideways to block it.

"I have the awful feeling that won't do us a lick of good this time," Angela murmured from just behind me. I flinched and turned around, seriously considering snarking at her for sneaking up on me. She gave me a tired little smile and squeezed my shoulder, and I moved over in my perch so she could see better.

That pre-dawn glow on my left grew stronger, losing some of its silvery-gray-greenish tinge. Taking on a rosy touch.

The first streaks of light from true dawn threaded through bare tree branches. I watched several lines of light creep across the lawns, between the houses.

Several sleepwalkers crossed the intersection, moving even more slowly, as if they were walking uphill on ice against a stiff wind. Soft, pale golden light spilled down the cross street of the intersection in a pillar at a forty-five-degree angle. The first sleepwalker to walk into it stumbled backward, then sort of spun around on one heel and went down. The next few that followed did the same.

More light speared between the houses further back along the trail the sleepwalkers followed. More walkers hit thin beams of light like they had run into a solid wall and staggered backward and went down. Then people stumbled into the light and went to their knees. When they hit the pavement and the sidewalk and the grass, they curled up, like potato bugs did when we poked them with grass or straw.

Then the sleepwalkers who had made it through the intersection slowly went to their knees, like marionettes being lowered to the stage. They wobbled and went down on their sides and curled up. The police officers in the patrol car opened their doors, slowly got out, and walked up to the closest people. I had to swallow down an urge to fling up the window and shout out to them to stop, to stay in their car, it had to be a trap. I never watched any of the *Walking Dead* episodes, but I could easily recognize this as a really good setup for them to get chomped on by undead creepy-crawlies.

We traced the progress of daylight dripping across the streets by the movements of people falling. The officers called for EMTs when nobody got up again, even after they nudged and checked pulses and tried to get people to sit up.

The arrival of dawn and daylight definitely had something to do with the sudden switch from horror TV episode to *Warehouse 13*. According to London and Sherwood, the ripples of unfriendly energy that registered as a kind of cyber itching stopped once light spilled across the ground. They registered a shimmering and a kind of thickening in the shield. There was a backwash of energy heading out through the weak spot that they speculated was being drained from the sleepwalkers. That ended as soon as dawn rolled across the landscape.

"So what does the dependence on darkness tell us about our enemy?" Ford said, once we had all reconvened inside Divine's.

Mum had taken over Angela's kitchen, whipping up one of her special breakfasts full of healing ingredients. We all gathered around, setting the table and figuring out what had happened.

"I have some ideas," Angela said slowly, "but this is beyond my particular experience or expertise. Such things are learned through facing them, and I have been blessed with allies who see the problems coming from a far distance and intervene in time. So the fact that my allies have not seen this, have not responded ..." She raised her head and locked gazes with Harry.

"Fae Realm stuff?" I guessed.

Harry blushed a little and went transparent around the edges. "Should I go check?" he said.

Angela just shook her head and murmured for us to relax and start breakfast without her, she was going to make a call.

Considering what I had glimpsed and requests I had made over the years, just in case, I figured she was going down to the Wishing Ball. It didn't hurt to signal Maurice to come out in the hall with me while everyone else was busy filling glasses, making toast, fetching things for Mum. He just nodded when I asked him if Angela was checking with Fae authorities or experts or whatever through the Wishing Ball. I was on the verge of asking him how exactly it worked, when he seemed to hear something and zipped away. Sometimes I didn't feel sorry for Maurice, shrunk down so small with limited magic, because he got around really well on those wings. Even if they were embarrassingly sparkly and gave off that cotton candy scent when he flew really fast.

I half-expected Angela to come back upstairs with that doctor friend of hers, who had checked me out before. The guy in the purple jogging suit and matching doctor's bag. I had a suspicion it would end up being like Mary Poppins' bag, with unlimited storage, able to take out one magical medical tool after another, until there was a huge pile sitting on the floor.

We were settling around the table, with the smells of cranberry-orange muffins and deluxe omelets and fried apples and hot chocolate making our stomachs rumble, when Angela returned. She had a very rare, single crease in her forehead, and her bottom lip looked a little swollen, like she had been gnawing on it.

"Bad news?" Ford got up to pull out a chair and held it for her.

"Bad news that disguises good news. We finally have an analysis off the particular resonance of the energy we're dealing with, trying to latch onto the shield and suck it dry." She sighed and reached for the big teapot with the unicorns and dragons painted on it. Her special recipe rejuvenating tea filled it. "When the energy of this weak place between realms and dimensions was harnessed and tamed, the previous guardian worked closely with powerful forces on the other side -- or I should say sides, plural -- of the weak spot. Your ancestress, Bethany, wove her personal power into the reinforcing, and if the good Lord is merciful, you will have enough magical potential inherited from your father's side, and from the blood your mother spilled defending Neighborlee, to help us. The bad news I received is that the resonance attacking the shield and energy is ancient Fae, as Harry theorized. Warped by time and malevolence. That is the weak spot in our defense. Even worse, the experts who followed the residue trail identified a bloodline the authorities believed, I daresay hoped strongly, had died out."

"I was afraid of that," Harry said. "The clues we were picking up reminded me of some bedtime stories my grandmother and nanny used to tell me. Rebel Fae, cast out into a sideways dimension. Kind of like the prison dimension in the opening sequence of *Superman*, you know? They were part of the justification for pulling back, reducing contact with the Human realm. They wanted to dominate, make Humans little more than pets, toys to manipulate and break as they chose. Their mistake was to start their campaign of domination by hunting down and slaughtering the half-bloods. To purify the bloodline. And shore up their insistence that Human blood automatically meant no magic whatsoever, that Humans couldn't perform magic or learn magic."

"That's been proven wrong," Lori said. "So very wrong. My grandfather and great-grandparents are cultural anthropologists and genealogists. Before I was born, they proved that the strongest magical bloodlines need regular infusions of Human blood to cleanse the weaknesses and problems that basically come from inbreeding. And some congenital problems inherent in living in the enclaves, with our freaky time warping."

"That's all fun and interesting," Kurt said, "but if these rebel Fae are showing up again, and dang if it doesn't make me think of the Dark Elves from the second Thor movie ... so we can expect these guys to try to get in and start making like Loki, thinking they're doing us a favor by taking away our freedom?"

"Taking away our intelligence and free will, among other things we value," Angela said.

"So what do we do? These guys aren't the kind who are going to retreat and lick their wounds for a few months or a year, gathering their strength, are they?" Pop said.

"We know who is coming after us now," Angela said. "And there are watchers posted on the other side of the weakness, prepared to counter the power that will be thrown at us. The sleepwalkers will walk again, like probes in a science fiction movie being sent to explore an alien environment. Or more accurately ..." She tipped her head back and studied the ceiling.

Or, I suddenly realized, she was studying or at least thinking about what was on the other side of the ceiling. One of the storage rooms on the third floor. Where Angela stored dangerous magical items.

"Turn off whatever is keeping them out? Turn off the electrical fence or the burglar alarms or something else that is keeping Divine's safe from invasion?" I guessed.

Angela flushed a little. "I really do need to join all of you in your movie marathon weekends. It is amazing and somewhat disconcerting how close to the truth your movie studios come to the eternal battle between realms. Yes, there is something hidden here, sleeping and paralyzed, that the rebels could believe they need to get their hands on, to crack the shield and tear open the doorway between realms. And I daresay many of the books stored here possess knowledge vital to their campaign to turn ordinary Humans into cattle to feed their ravenous hunger for power and pain and fear."

A chiming went through the house. I flinched, and Angela gave me a strange look that was half guilty, half amused.

"What was that?" I didn't care that my voice cracked.

"Doorbell," Maurice said, and zipped out of the room. I assumed he was heading downstairs to see who was there.

"Okay … front door, or one of those doors we're not supposed to see?"

"Front door," Angela said. She sighed and rubbed at her temples. "I'm sorry, Lanie. Whatever we went through yesterday changed something in you. Knocked something loose, or perhaps more accurately, into alignment, so you're more sensitive to the energies and resonances that you escaped experiencing all this time."

"So basically what Kurt and Jane and Portia pick up on?"

Before she could answer, Maurice darted back into the room, proving just how fast he could move, despite being smaller than a Barbie doll, thanks to his wings. He reported that Gordon was at the door. It had to be pretty serious if he was showing up, instead of calling. Something else had happened last night, besides the walkers converging on the west side of Overlook.

The "something else" turned out to be a fire.

At the flower shop.

Witnesses saw several big black dogs with glowing eyes running in and out, through the burning walls, through multicolored flames. Supposedly, those big dogs were the size of horses. The witnesses were college kids who had gone looking for a safe place to party. The responding officers originally came in response to 911 calls about screams and explosions and flashes of light. Several calls reported a car on fire in the parking lot of the old flower shop. One call came from a member of Cutterville City

Council who reminded the dispatcher, and wanted it on record, that he had been trying to have the building torn down for the past five years. Neighborlee police and fire weren't called at first, because the flower shop was in Cutterville and the calls came from residents on the other side of the woods that surrounded the shop. Neighborlee became involved when the witnesses were identified as Willis-Brooks College students who lived off-campus, which made them Neighborlee's responsibility. They were found huddled in the questionable shelter of the woods, watching the shop and one of their cars burn. The untouched car had enough hard liquor and illegal prescription drugs and homemade drugs to explain why the college kids saw the big dogs with glowing eyes.

"Well, that explains why the Hounds didn't come with me," Dawn said. "I had an impression from them that they were furious ..." She shrugged and gave a weak, guilty-looking grin to Gordon. "You don't really want an explanation, do you?"

"No." He sighed. "That place has been a problem, and the Chief said off the record he's glad it's been handled. He sure hopes the investigation doesn't point to anyone on our side of the street." He gave Angela a hopeful, weary look. Poor Gordon had probably been up all night and stopped on his way home to report.

"It shouldn't," she said. "What sort of investigation?"

"Well, it would normally just be the Cutterville Fire Department, the arson squad maybe. The thing is, the responding officers confirmed the flames were all sorts of colors, and they heard weird noises, and there was this black ooze coming out from the building in a few spots and the smells weren't the normal smells you'd expect from an old building burning down. They're calling in ATF and the EPA, and maybe the DEA if they find the wrong sort of stuff in the ashes and the solidified goo. If it solidifies." He shuddered a little and raked one hand through his sweaty hair.

We found out later the EPA was indeed called in to investigate the sludge found on the premises. If the owner of the property wasn't in trouble for illegal and unsafe storage practices, he would be in trouble for not securing his property to keep others from using it for illegal and unsafe practices and purposes.

"So can we assume the Hounds did a really thorough housecleaning?" Pop said, once Gordon had gone home. Angela gave him a big packet of one of her specialty teas, to help him sleep and to cleanse his blood from anything unfriendly he might have inhaled while surveying the scene of the fire.

He had showed us pictures of the site. The place looked like it had been through a couple dozen disaster movies. The rubble looked melted, and the camera hadn't caught the hint of phosphorescent glow Gordon had reported. He was relieved that other officers at the scene had been able to see it as well. There was more damage there than could be explained away by a really hot fire, even if the place had been storing all sorts of illegal chemicals and other substances. At one point, the flames had swirled together into a funnel cloud and everything had gone up in the air with a roaring whoosh, like a weird kind of controlled explosion.

Kurt and Jane made arrangements to take Angela, Harry and Lori to examine the site, once things had cooled down. Literally and figuratively. We needed to know just what the Hounds had done and if some nasty doorways to the Fae Realms or other dimensions had been closed up. Maybe nailed shut. Maybe melted shut, or at least blocked with the magical equivalent of welding. Kind of like that scene in *X-Men: Days of Future Past*, when they blocked the doorway to the temple to keep the Sentinels out.

Not exactly a good image, because no matter what Professor X and Magneto and the others did, the Sentinels got inside.

"We will be grateful for whatever steps they took," Angela said slowly. "However ..."

"There's always a however," Kurt muttered. I knew he was trying to lighten the mood, but we were all too tired and headachy to appreciate it or be helped much.

"The Hounds are not of our dimension, our realms. They may have done great good or they may have just ..." She sighed. "Exacerbated and exasperated the situation. They were entirely in their right to attack because the threat focused on Dawn, who is their responsibility. Yet when combatants from two different realities and wars clash, sometimes the results are not what we perceive them or want them to be."

"So get ready for round two?" Maurice said.

"The shop was their entrance point, their headquarters, their power base. They could be rendered powerless. They could also be stirred up to a point of fury and desperation that will make them unpredictable. And we have no way of knowing where they will attack. While the shop was there, we could at least trace the power attacking us back to that point."

"Sorry," Dawn whispered.

"You are not to blame." She stepped over to the sofa where Dawn had curled up, looking like she wanted to shrink down and vanish, and gripped her shoulders. "Never blame yourself for choices made in situations where you have no grounding or preparation. No matter what, the enemy was indeed dealt a serious blow last night. We simply need to prepare for every possible reaction and contingency."

Through Harry and the Wishing Ball, Angela sent a request for experts in Fae magic to also come and investigate the site of the flower shop, to determine the outcome of the Hounds' attack. It would help if they could determine if a doorway had been forced open between Earth and whatever sideways or pocket dimension Kerri and her minions had been hiding in. Getting those answers would take time. There was no telling how long it would take to assemble a team to handle the investigation. If a team came at all. There was no telling with Fae politics. And wasn't that a little frustrating, and far too familiar a situation?

"I admit," Angela said, "I will sleep better at night, knowing that particular malevolent spot has been wiped away, physically and metaphysically, with another enemy no longer perched on the border, beyond our authority and reach, watching us."

"Trying to watch us," Maurice corrected. "I think with all the fumbles they've been making, and all the blind swatting, they proved they didn't know where to aim or even what or who they were aiming at."

"Until last night," Ford said, giving Angela a concerned look.

"Yes," she said, nodding slowly. "Until last night." She sighed. "Lanie, call Pastor Rocky as soon as you think he's awake, and ask him to call in the strongest and loudest prayer warriors, would you? We're going to need all the help and support we can get."

I did just that.

We discussed more situations and things we had learned over the last couple years as we finished the incredible breakfast Mum made. The attempt to get hold of a book full of imprisoned magic last year, which had brought Troy and Diane Richards together, could now be traced to the rebel Fae. Defeating the Rivals and restoring the magical energy reservoir had turned out to work against us, because it made Neighborlee and the doorways it controlled easier to find, easier to target from different dimensions.

"We shouldn't be discouraged," Angela said. "This could be part of the master plan to resolve the problem of the enemies we have struggled against for decades. The important thing is to search and examine everything I have held in trust and have kept sleeping, and determine what is dangerous to us, and what can help us. Chances are very good that the rebel Fae want to and need to get inside the barriers and restraints anchored in place by Divine's Emporium, to access something that will unleash power for their use, tear open gates, and knock down walls between dimensions. We must also be ready for the sleepwalkers to return. The coming of dawn halted their activities this morning, and perhaps dawn will halt them again tomorrow, but eventually they will grow strong enough that daylight will not harm them. That is something we must avoid at all costs, because we are, after all, the servants and the forces of light."

Chapter Fifteen

At Christmas, I had gotten a glimpse of the Ether Lexicon, the repository of all Fae knowledge and history. Harry, Lori and Bethany went to the Miller house to do some heavy-duty cramming and searching of the Lexicon, reading the Fae version of faerie tales to do research. They couldn't do it at Divine's because Maurice was there. Part of his exile meant he couldn't access the Ether Lexicon, so it wouldn't show up if he was nearby. He offered to spend the day at the library with Holly, to get out of the way. Angela told him she needed his help in ransacking the storage rooms on the third floor used to keep magical items sleeping and relatively harmless. Despite his reduced magic, he still had strong sensitivity, and he would be our Geiger counter to locate any magical items that might benefit the rebel Fae.

Asmondius showed up to confer with London and Sherwood. It was kind of funny to discover that they couldn't see or hear him, even though he sat in front of the computers where they manifested for the conference. Athena and Wallace had to act as interpreters. They would have been needed to interpret even if Asmondius could be heard and seen by cameras and microphones. There was all the technical jargon he couldn't understand, and despite the massive fantastical fiction reading the two AI's had been doing for fun, there were cultural references and magical terminology they either didn't know or couldn't understand. Athena and Wallace translated for both sides. They could think of examples and illustrations far more quickly than our two AI's were able to search their massive databases.

We got an update from Chief Tanner mid-afternoon, after all the sleepwalkers had been checked out at the hospital. Everyone had pretty much the same story. Weird dreams of being lost and trying to find their way out of some big, dark, echoing place, with the impression of something coming up behind them. They had to find the source of a far distant light and get inside, to be safe from something that growled and made the ground shake as it got closer.

Everyone had dangerously low levels of minerals in their blood. The medical staff sent them all home with nutritional supplements and painkillers to deal with their massive headaches. The walkers on the east side of Overlook had never suffered these physical symptoms. Then again, they hadn't collapsed, either. Much more than we had at first guessed had changed in our enemies' strategies and methods last night. More proof this needed to be stopped as soon as possible.

The walkers' families were instructed to keep an eye on them, make sure they didn't leave their homes, and call the authorities if they got out. The hospital wanted to keep them for observation, but didn't have room to house them all. If the hospital couldn't keep them all, it couldn't keep any. Everyone had follow-up appointments for EEGs and MRIs and other tests, once the results of more intensive blood tests came in. Plus, there were all the requests to search for things like gas leaks, something odd in the water, or something tainted that all the walkers had eaten, to determine what was to blame for the walking.

The line of "enough" had been crossed, and something had to be done. Even if all the tests to determine a physical, biological reason were a waste of time. We certainly couldn't tell the walkers or the authorities that they were being used by magical enemies from another dimension to break down the door that Neighborlee had kept sealed for centuries.

Divine's budded enough rooms for all of us to curl up and take power naps after our long breakfast. There was a lot of work to do, and chances were good the walkers would return, once night had come. None of us napped very long.

By dinnertime, Harry, Bethany and Lori had found five, just five stories in the historical and literature chronicles that talked about the tactics and tricks of the rebel Fae. They reported each discovery to Asmondius and Angela.

Kurt, Jane, Ford and Portia drove around the border of town, testing for any weak spots, fluctuations, and even tears in the shield. Lori's Brick used what influence he had with the authorities to get information on the fire at the flower shop. Cosmo and Doni and my folks got to work researching, trying to track down faerie tales that might be helpful in anticipating what the rebel Fae would do, as well as digging into the history of the flower shop, the buildings that had been on that piece of property down through the centuries, and the land itself. Every little blip of weirdness would help, offering us a clue, a hint, and yes, a new rabbit trail to investigate.

I was part of the team ransacking the storage rooms on the third floor. When we broke for dinner, we had gone through a little less than three-quarters of the contents of the first room, and Maurice had only flagged three items that made him itch with some residue of Fae energy. If we could have just opened a box and had Maurice hover over the contents, we could have gotten through two rooms by mid-afternoon. However, the boxes Angela used for storing each magical item enforced the hibernation, muffling magical potential and threat. We had to take the items out of the boxes and move them out of the storage room, which also had a muffling and hibernation effect.

My telekinesis had been affected slightly by being in the tug-of-war with the doppelganger, but I still had enough strength and control to help with the search. That was a good thing, because we didn't dare touch the items with even gloved hands. The chance of something being irritated at being awakened from sleep, and lashing out at whoever was touching them, was too big to risk.

The process was time-consuming, with so many cautious steps. I sat in the doorway of the storage room. Angela opened each box and held it out where I could see the contents. I picked up the contents with telekinesis, and flew it out into the hallway, to land on the table where Felicity and Maurice were stationed. Felicity was there as a stopgap, to zap anything that woke up cranky. Maurice waited until the residue of the hibernation field in the storage room wore off, then tested the item. Larger items took longer to come clean and reveal their nature and energy levels. We averaged six items tested in an hour.

I wanted to get back to work after dinner, but Angela insisted we all needed to get some sleep. Night was already falling, and we needed to take what rest and recuperation we could while we waited for the magical energy to build up in the people our enemy would try to influence tonight. The longer it took for sleepwalkers to take to the streets, the better for us.

After their conference with Asmondius, London and Sherwood had gotten to work refining their monitoring system for the defensive shield. Kurt and Ford spent a few hours in Kurt's workshop, upgrading the sensors they had devised, and embedded in the ground wherever they could, all around the borders of Neighborlee. They wanted double the number of sensors, to build up the coverage. However, that only meant that instead of one sensor spike every twenty feet, we now had them ten feet apart, and there were too many places where it was impossible to pound a spike into the ground, because of roads and private property with fences around them, and businesses. It was amazing, and irritating, how many buildings straddled the borders of two cities. While the men were tinkering and building, Portia and Jane continued patrolling and monitoring. That was especially important once afternoon slid toward evening. There was no telling when the enemy would resume drilling through the shield to reach the next batch of puppets to send staggering down the sidewalks and streets to Divine's.

If we were lucky and there was no attack tonight, Kurt and Ford would build and bury more sensors tomorrow. And the next day. Until we had a solid wall of sensors reinforcing the shield, into which the AI's would feed all the energy they could harvest. Once evening approached, they gathered up food and hot drinks and headed out to meet up with Portia and Jane, to feed them and resume monitoring the borders of our town.

The most important part of the sensors' function, besides helping London and Sherwood send cyber dimension energy into the shield, was to make it easier for them to change the resonance of the shield and make it harder to penetrate.

The only problem was that constantly changing the resonance could establish a pattern that would become predictable, as well as waste energy. The AI's planned to wait until they knew the shield was under attack, then start tinkering.

Pastor Rocky called just before we sat down to eat dinner, to ask about the "situation" and if there were any new or special concerns. He assured us the prayer warrior teams had been hard at work, praying for us and "pestering" God on our behalf.

I said a prayer, thanking God we had him on our side. I shuddered a little to think what kind of reaction a pastor in a church outside Neighborlee would be having to hearing even a fraction of what we went through on a regular basis. The most extreme reaction would be to call in an exorcist, or health authorities to make sure we weren't being poisoned by toxic waste in the water and air, or someone hadn't put hallucinogens in the water supply.

We lay down to rest after dinner, but I doubt anyone slept. We knew the attack wouldn't start at nightfall. The enemy had established a pattern. They needed time to gather their influence and power. They needed to send their energy and influence to the sleepwalkers and have it build up before the walking started. They had to get through the shield, for one thing. We were ready to not just reinforce that shield, but attack.

Just because we knew we had time didn't let us relax.

Soon, we headed up to the storage room to finish going through the items. Everything Maurice had detected with the right magical resonance so far had been turned over to Asmondius, to deal with. We had to trust that getting those items out of the shop would cut down on the attraction and the vulnerability of Divine's, if the enemy actually succeeded in breaching the defenses.

We fully intended to do everything necessary to prevent that. At the same time, I wasn't sure what that would entail, if it came down to a do-or-die moment. It wasn't just Earth depending on us, and the questionable freedom and safety of the Human race, but possibly opening a gateway to multiple other dimensions. And maybe reigniting that ancient war in the Fae Realms.

Yeah, just put a little too much pressure on us, why don't you?

Gordon was on duty in the dispatch room of the police station that night. He volunteered. He called just after midnight to let us know that four families of sleepwalkers had contacted the central number to report their walkers had tried to leave the house. That was later than the previous nights. What did that mean?

We found that answer, less than ten minutes after Gordon reported in.

Ford and Jake were out driving patrol through the most heavily populated streets where the sleepwalkers had originated. They focused on the addresses where the sleepwalkers didn't have family members in the houses with them, and they had been most resistant to the advice of the doctors about preventing sleepwalking again. Of course, the doctors didn't know the real reasons, so that advice probably wouldn't have worked anyway. They encountered six walkers and used the same techniques we had been using on the other side of Overlook Drive, to try to turn them back.

It worked.

For a while.

They blocked the path of the walkers, waited until they had turned around and headed back the way they had come, then moved on. They came back after dealing with two other walkers, each, to find the walkers they had already turned back had turned around again and were back on track, heading for Divine's. That was new and discouraging.

Then Kurt called in.

"I can see power lines. It's not little peppering strikes, it's steady streams. Very thin, phasing in and out. It's freaky how we can see the energy of the shield around the weak spot where the invading energy is passing through. It's like they're starting to pulse in synch."

"Matching resonance," Angela theorized, when I passed on what Kurt had told us. "On the positive side, we know where the attack is being focused."

My phone rang again, like her words were a signal.

"Something is coming," Jane said, before I could even say hello. "We want to try something. Feel like painting another target on your back?"

So that was how I ended up driving to the weak spot that hadn't entirely healed from last night's assault: the street right in front of the main parking lot of Neighborlee High School, within sight of the wreckage of the flower shop.

That answered one question and killed a hope we had. Destroying the old building hadn't severed the trans-dimensional connection and hadn't uprooted the anchor for the enemy's operations.

Felicity came with me. Kurt's plan was for me to show my face and tempt the enemy to make a strike at me. We knew I wasn't the ultimate target, but the fact the enemy had tried to get hold of me several times now made the odds good they would try again, and through me get at Angela. The worst-case scenario had me taken over, like a host carrying an alien in my belly into Neighborlee. When Angela joined the effort to free me, the enemy would burst out and attack her.

Not on my watch.

Kurt wanted to try to finish the scorching that had taken place two days ago. He needed me as bait and to borrow my telekinesis. We needed Felicity for her EM bursts to bolster the shield, hopefully, and fry the enemy badly enough it would either destroy itself, or give up and go away with its tail between its legs -- if it had a tail and legs, because I was envisioning it as some kind of octopus thing, maybe an airborne kraken, or a living Hydra symbol.

When we arrived in the school parking lot, I saw a shimmering, rippling kind of wall of dark-tinted light, fading in and out, with a few veins or what looked like spider webbing through it, surrounding a glowing circle with a handful of strings extending from it. Honestly, they looked like those shampoo commercials showing scaly hairs. Kurt theorized those strings were lines of power coming from the enemy. They were rough, segmented, scaley, and I imagined the scales digging into my skin if I got my hands on them to pull. Not that I wanted to touch them.

"That's brilliant," Kurt said, when I was stupid enough to voice what I was thinking. "Why wait for it to come to us?" Then he did a doubletake. "You can see it?"

"Yeah." I looked at Felicity. "Can you?"

Kurt and I groaned when Felicity shook her head.

"Maybe you got rewired or you got something shifted around when that thing tried to drain you," Jane theorized. "Can you feel the vibrations now?" She rubbed her fingers together.

I paused to think, and to "listen" through more than my ears. Yeah, I could feel a thrumming in the tips of my fingers, in the soles of my feet, that synched perfectly with the brightening pulses of those strings of invading energy.

"Can you get your mental hands on those strings?" Kurt said, once I reported what I could now feel.

"Why?" My physical hands itched. I didn't want to touch that stuff, after the close encounter I had gone through the other day.

"That thing got scorched when we pulled you, physically, away from the border and it was trying to pull you through to its side. What if we pulled it into the shield? We'd have to do it fast, so it didn't have time to let go and escape. And maybe if it's attached to those lines, it can't break free."

"Go for it." Felicity held up her hands, fingers spread. Sparks danced across her fingertips. "I really need to incinerate something."

Before we did anything, we checked in with Divine's. Since I was the bait, I couldn't be in the middle of a conversation when the enemy hit. Kurt and Jane were monitoring the sensors and watching the approach of what they described as a big, churning glob of energy. They could see it, I couldn't. Which just went to prove that although I could see some energy, I couldn't see it all. Yet. Who knew what other changes would occur in my and everyone else's semi-pseudo-superpowers by the time this current crisis was over?

So that left Felicity to be our communications officer. While she was on the phone, checking in with Angela and getting Gordon's update on a dozen more sleepwalkers fighting to escape their families, Jake showed up. Nobody had told him Felicity had left Divine's. He just knew. That was true love. He had been through enough with us over the last two years, he didn't even raise an eyebrow when we told him what we could see and sense, and what we planned to do.

"You know, with this immunity of Daniel's, it might be smart to call him, add him to the mix." He kept his gaze locked on Felicity, who was bent over the hood of my Jeep, writing down everything being passed on from Gordon.

"Well, that was stupid," Kurt muttered. He looked at me and grinned. "I was just starting to think this was like old times, the three of us against the boogiemen, but it's not just us anymore."

"It never was," I had to say. But I understood what he meant.

"Yeah, but when we were kids ..." He sighed. "I think we're finally growing up, willing to admit we can't save the world by ourselves. You'd better make the call," he said to Jake. "We don't need Lanie to be on the phone when the attack comes. All hands on deck."

"It's speeding up," Jane said, before Jake had done more than say hello to Daniel.

"Just now, or did it start when Lanie got here?" Kurt glanced over his shoulder at me. I was behind them about twenty feet, next to my Jeep, with Felicity sitting on the hood and Jake on her other side, talking.

"A little bit. Hard to separate from the normal acceleration we were noting before you called with your plan," Jane said, sounding a little distracted. "Going up."

"When did it start accelerating?" he called, as Jane went up and went semi-transparent. '

This late at night, there was less need for caution like going invisible. We were far enough away from any houses that if we talked in normal voices, nobody would hear us.

"I suppose that was when I got close enough to be sensed," Angela said.

She stepped out of the darkness, into the parking lot light about twenty feet to our right, with Ford, Jinx, Portia, and Jane's friend from Hoax, Katie, who could run at super-sonic speeds. I had the feeling that was how they got to the school so fast.

"Angela, you can't," Kurt said.

"We tried to tell her," Ford said with a shrug. "Son, I've been fighting her on some issues of doing our job twice as long as you've been alive. I learned to give up about forty years ago, whenever she gets that look in her eye that she's got now."

"If Lanie is good bait, I'm even better." Angela crossed to take position next to my chair. She rested her hand on my shoulder. "That warped thing that used to be a Fae got a taste of both of us, that's how it's able to focus the sleepwalkers. I'm hoping that once I left, Divine's ceased being a target. In the final analysis, it's far more important than I am. The two of us here should help to focus the enemy on this spot. We all need to be together to fight it."

"Yeah, but do we want it focused completely?" Felicity said. "Angela, what do we do if anything happens to you?"

"If we can't fight that thing back now, tonight, once and for all," Portia said, "or at least give it a good whooping so it really does go away to regroup for a few years ..." She shrugged and exchanged a weary look with her father. "Well, chances are good none of us are going to see the sunrise. I'm not being a pessimist, but as someone who can read quite a lot of inimical energy, that thing coming at us is investing everything it has on breaking through. We can't do any less. We win tonight, or there isn't any tomorrow for any of us."

I didn't dare argue with her. She had given up raising Athena to keep her daughter safe. She had remained hidden from the Rivals, and traveled the world, searching for signs of other Lost Kids and weak spots in the barrier between realms. Portia didn't have a lot of active powers, but she was an expert, and that was hard-won knowledge paid for by a high price. We had to trust she knew what she was talking about.

"Almost here!" Jane called. "Gaining speed geometrically. Felicity, can you give us a boost?"

Felicity bared her teeth, crossed her arms over her chest, and stepped out, away from my Jeep a good fifteen feet. I appreciated that. She had learned a lot of control over her EM bursts, but tonight with so much at stake, she might slip and zap any electronics nearby. Not that I would blame her.

Green and pink and blue sparks swirled through Felicity's hair, then streamed down her shoulders and spun around her body, going faster as they spiraled down to her feet and then up again. The vortex of energy spun out, splitting into two streamers that went to Kurt and Jane. He spread his arms and shot up in the air to hang there, even with Jane, about ten feet apart. Directly below them, the sensor stakes sparked and hummed and pulsed, bright then dim, bright then dim, like a heartbeat.

Dimly behind me, I heard the teletype sound of a text message.

"Sleepwalkers have changed course," Ford called out. "Wallace and the rest of the kids took up patrol for us, and they're tracking them. Probably headed this way."

Chapter Sixteen

I felt sick for a moment, thinking of Overlook Drive. It had kept the east side of the street sleepwalkers from crossing to Divine's side of town. Would the walkers on the west side try to cross? Would we have some fatalities at long last? Not that there was much traffic to be noticed. Certainly the few cars that had gone by since I arrived at the high school hadn't noticed the lights flaring and dimming along the street. Would they notice anything once the real light show started?

The streamers of energy hit the globes of the Ghost field around Kurt and Jane, making them flare.

Another text. Ford reported the energy streams going through the weak spot were thickening, according to Sherwood.

Silent lightning struck the shield in front of us. I felt that *thud-sproing* reverberation that always felt kind of silly in movies, when rockets and meteors hit force fields. I always thought all that energy being hit by a solid object should have resulted in an explosion, not a rebound like hitting something half-metal and half-rubber.

Portia let out a choked cry. When the sparks from the lightning strike faded from my eyes, I saw what she saw, and nearly let out a yelp myself. It was dang ugly, for one thing. It looked like a whirlwind of tattered sheets, with ghost features -- black eyes, black nose, black streak for a mouth. At the same time, it looked melted. No, a second later I corrected that -- it was still melting. Trying to heal, because among the whipping, swirling strands of black and white rags, I saw features trying to morph into place over the decaying shreds. I saw my own face a few times, Daniel's face, other people's faces.

The thing was huge, hovering in mid-air over the dividing line of the street between Neighborlee and Cutterville. It grew taller, wider, with every heartbeat that passed, and sparks and shreds of debris, street trash, the charred remains of the old flower shop building, were being gathered to it, making up its mass. From the movement of that black smear of mouth, I had the feeling it was shrieking curses at us, but I couldn't hear anything. I didn't want to hear anything. Whatever it said would probably scorch our ears and our minds.

The mama of all doppelgangers hung there, gathering itself to smash the shield, reach through, and grab us. It was looking right at me -- but only because I was right next to Angela. Common sense said Angela and Divine's would always be the target.

"London says the streams are thickening, forcing the weak spot to widen," Ford yelled up to Kurt and Jane.

He was right. The energy strings did look thicker. My hands itched just thinking about grabbing those things and pulling, if we had to follow through on Kurt's plan. Whatever it was. He really hadn't explained all the details, had he?

"Pincer move!" Jane shouted.

She and Kurt held out their hands to each other, positioning their defensive globes on either side of the strings, then smashed in toward each other, pressing them flat. For a few seconds, they flickered and seemed to go out.

Outside the shield, the shred monster jerked and writhed and kicked its legs. It slammed down against the shield. Silver and green sparks shot up in the air. It arched its back and I felt its deep howl of pain even if I couldn't hear with my physical ears.

"It's connected," I shouted up to Jane and Kurt. "It's tied to the power strings. When you smashed the strings, you smashed it."

"That's what we were hoping for," Kurt shouted back. He and Jane pressed in closer to each other, sending up sparks as they smashed the strings even further.

The monster howled and kicked and jerked as the energy strings pulled it down against the shield again.

"Lanie, pull!"

I launched myself from my chair and rose about ten feet up to the strings. Then I reached with my hands, physical and mental, and wrapped everything I had around that single, pulsing, throbbing stream of power connecting to the shred monster.

Yeah, it hurt. It was as jagged to the touch as it looked. I felt it with my body and my mind.

It took a bite out of me in return. My hands burned like a thousand mosquitos landed on me all at once and dug their stingers into me with one unified stab. Through the sparks swirling around my eyes, I saw the shred monster glowing brighter.

I had one second to think that Kurt had finally messed up, had theorized wrong, in the biggest, worst way possible.

Then he took over my telekinesis. His and Jane's energy enfolded and insulated me. I felt Felicity's EM power. It wasn't so much a physical sensation as a smell, and it smelled like her when she was happy, of vanilla and cinnamon and clean laundry on the line.

Together, we pulled, hard, dragging ourselves backward telekinetically and physically. I dropped down into my chair and reached with another mental hand to anchor myself to the ground. The doppelganger mama writhed and kicked and screamed, and yeah, the sounds lashed and clawed at my soul instead of my ears, and it was nasty. Sparks fountained up where it slapped against the shield. It kicked, it lunged up in the air. It clawed at the energy strings, all tangled into a twisting cord, trying to cut itself free.

We weren't letting that happen.

The globes of the Ghost field around Kurt and Jane flared bright, reflecting on the people around us. I heard Ford shouting something, probably readings on the shield coming from Sherwood, but couldn't make out the words.

A huge, vicious yank pulled me out of my chair. I was in the air, rising upward despite my mental anchor to the ground, jerked back and forth, mirroring the doppelganger mama's efforts to break free. Felicity screamed my name and Jake leaped to catch hold of my feet. He pulled down hard, so I thought he might yank my feet off at the ankles.

Then we were both in the air. The doppelganger moved away, upward.

"Ain't gonna happen!" Kurt growled, and the Ghost field flared even brighter.

I had a sudden awful vision of getting pulled up high enough to bang against the inside of the shield. Would I get scorched? Or would I be recognized as a friendly resident, and allowed through? What would happen if I left Neighborlee and had nothing between me and the shred monster?

"Please ..." I whispered, with the strength of all the prayers I had been praying ever since this whole bizarre problem showed itself. I closed my eyes and reached down a second mental hand for the ground. It dug through the parking lot pavement, through the soil, into the foundation stone of Neighborlee. I sank mental and emotional anchors and I pulled down hard with everything I had.

Ford shouted something about rising levels and London trying something with the intake, but I had no idea what either of them meant. I couldn't spare the attention or energy to think.

A horrendous shriek vibrated through the energy stream. It yanked my eyes open, in time to see Kurt and Jane pull down hard with holographic projections of their arms, their enlarged fists wrapped around the throat and the waist of the doppelganger mama. One huge, fierce yank, and it smashed down into the shield.

The shield flared. It dipped, bending inward, resisting the entrance of the shred monster. Everyone around me let out shouts and winced and raised their hands to shield their eyes. Somehow, I kept my eyes open, stunned and yet not blinded as ugly, greeny-black-infected red light flared up where the doppelganger mama smashed up against, then *through* the shield. That poisoned light brightened, turning gold and then silver-white. An audible shriek wailed through the air. The really frightening part was that something about it sounded familiar.

I am not joking. It sounded so much like the howling wail of the Wicked Witch of the West, I thought I heard the equivalent of, "I'll get you, my pretty. And your little dog too!"

"My pretty" being Angela. And "your little dog" meaning all of us who had gathered to do whatever it took to protect her.

The doppelganger mama disintegrated only a few feet inside the shield, raining down sparks on us. At first, the smell was like the stink of a dumpster on a hot, humid summer day with rotting garbage a foot deep inside. Then that sodden reek turned into the bitterness of ashes.

The energy strings snapped. I fell. Only about eight feet, but I was in no condition to try to land smart. I couldn't use my telekinesis to cushion myself, because I felt absolutely burned hollow. I landed on my side, one knee caught underneath me, and I rolled, ending up sprawled on my back. And yeah, slammed the back of my head against the pavement. Fortunately, just short of slamming into one of those parking lot bumpers.

We all just lay or sat where we had landed, in the dark, because hey, guess what? Our battle had produced a rolling blackout for about eight blocks in every direction from the parking lot. We found that out later from Gordon and Chief Tanner. The tug-of-war with the doppelganger mama also burst about two-thirds of the light bulbs and florescent tubes in the high school and flipped nearly every breaker.

None of us cared. We just sat or lay there in the darkness, trying to remember how to breathe. Some of us were afraid we had been struck blind by the light show. There was some whimpering, and I honestly couldn't say if it came from me or someone else. Maybe several someone elses. A lot of groaning. Then some laughing, really ragged, the kind where you have to laugh because otherwise you're going to cry, and it's too wonderful to know you're still alive to give in to tears.

Athena, Wallace, Cosmo, Doni, and Dawn got to us first. They had already been on their way as soon as they determined that yes, the sleepwalkers were heading for the high school. Right on their heels were Daniel and a dozen cars full of Sheridan people, armed with healers and blankets and hot coffee. Athena checked in with London and Sherwood on her computer. Our cars and all our electronic gear were fried. The new sensors Kurt and Ford had installed provided London some very interesting results before they fried.

And then, of course, it started raining. That kind of made sense, because we had been messing with natural and supernatural and otherworldly energies and that had to have an unbalancing effect on the physical realm.

The most important detail in the aftermath and cleanup, which kind of gave us the energy to tell our aching bodies to shut up and get us out of there: the tug-of-war and subsequent incineration of the monster had recharged the shield. When the shred monster went up in sparks and smoke, that released a lot of energy, and London harvested it all.

The doppelganger was definitely dead. Not just scorched and running away to lick its wounds and prepare for the second wave. London and Sherwood had identified several dozen power lines reaching out from the monster to its minions, which it was using as batteries, sucking power from them. London backtracked those lines and effectively slapped patches on the ones she couldn't essentially shut down or try to program to leave us alone.

Even more important, and encouraging -- and when we thought about it, a little irritating, because shouldn't they have been fighting alongside us? -- Asmondius reported a large number of Fae defenders and historians and officials had been watching from the other side of the dimensional barriers. They were there to jump in and take advantage of weaknesses and any second wave of rebel Fae who might strike while we needed to move back and catch our breaths. Fortunately, we never did, according to Asmondius. He spoke to us from inside the Wishing Ball that morning, after another of Mum's huge, healing feasts. Kind of weird, talking to just a head in a purple haze. He congratulated us on the speedy and efficient dispatching of the rebel Fae and appropriating nearly all the power they had hoarded and warped over centuries of preparation. They had effectively been thrown back to square one, according to the experts. Yeah, but how sure could those so-called experts be, when they hadn't had to deal with the rebel Fae in centuries -- their centuries, not Human centuries? And seriously? That was a fast battle? In some aspects, it felt like we were fighting for days, if not months. Yet according to those watching and even critiquing our fighting style and our command of our superhero powers, it took less than twenty minutes once the doppelganger mama showed up and we started the tug-of-war.

As far as any of us were concerned, the fate of Earth, all Human life, and maybe a dozen other realms hanging in the balance for twenty minutes was nineteen minutes and fifty seconds too long.

Fortunately, this time around the sleepwalkers didn't collapse. And none of them got as far as Overlook Drive, so we didn't have to worry about late night/early morning drivers hitting anyone. Once the tug-of-war started, the doppelganger mama lost her grasp on the sleepwalkers. Some of them woke up, and they weren't very happy to find themselves outside, in their pajamas or underwear and bare feet, just as a storm rolled in. At least, they thought it was a storm, all that lightning in the sky and the rumbling of very strange thunder. It drove them to run for home in a panic. The ones who didn't wake up went home again like they had homing signals and didn't wake up when the actual rain fell and drenched some of them. They did wake up when they tried to get into their houses, and some of them were locked out, while others found their families surrounding them, shouting with relief. In a few cases they had locked the sleepwalkers out of the house and had called the police. Too many people in Neighborlee, it appeared, had been watching zombie movies and weren't too sure they wanted to let the sleepwalkers back in until they had been examined and were cleared of any viruses or tendencies to snack on living flesh.

The rain started while the Sheridan people were getting all of us into their cars. Because, as stated before, all our cars were dead. Even Kurt's fix-it talent couldn't get them going. After breakfast and getting checked by the Sheridan healers and getting the report of the Fae side of the battle from Asmondius, we went back to the high school parking lot. This time, all our cars worked perfectly fine. They just needed time to recover. Weird.

Daniel got me excused from going to work. Glory and hallelujah. All I wanted to do was sleep.

Arthur Sheridan got his PR and legal people together and took care of a lot of the cleanup problems when it came to the sleepwalkers and the hospital people who were involved, and dealing with Chief Tanner. Nice, because none of us were up to the mental and emotional task of coming up with answers and cover stories.

We all needed our rest, because we weren't quite so naïve and optimistic that we didn't expect any retaliatory actions over the next few nights. We were on alert, flying patrols, looking for sleepwalkers, sitting vigils at computers and monitoring the shield. Just in case there was some reserve of rebel Fae energy that didn't get soaked up and used up and incinerated along with doppelganger mama. We devised a routine of going to bed right after supper and sleeping until full dark. Then we took our positions until dawn. Then we caught a few hours of sleep, got to work and school late, took power naps at lunch, and repeated the process the next night.

However, we hadn't even started to get used to that routine when word came from the Fae side of the problem. They had followed the power trail back to the pocket dimension where the rebel Fae had been hiding and gathering their strength and plotting for all those centuries. Their numbers were seriously decimated. The effort had drained them, to the point they had used up their own lives. Their power levels were down, their home was a wreck, and nearly uninhabitable from the backlash. The rebel Fae had gambled everything and lost.

So even though Asmondius congratulated us and told us we had the gratitude of the Fae realms and their allies and advised us to relax and enjoy the quiet time, we couldn't. We knew we didn't dare.

Divine's Emporium would always be a target. Angela would always be a target. We had been taught an important lesson of just how desperate and determined enemy forces could be to take over, break through, and destroy the barrier and the keeper of the doorway.

We were the guardians, and even though we gladly let loose and celebrated a little bit, we would never fully relax. Even though spring was coming and spring break was nearly on us. At least Maurice could relax and run off with Holly and enjoy his spring equinox one full day of being full-size, visible, audible, sans wings.

Guardians had learned long ago, after all, to appreciate the little joys in life.

END

About the Author

On the road to publication, Michelle fell into fandom in college and has 40+ stories in various SF and fantasy universes. She has a bunch of useless degrees in theater, English, film/communication, and writing. Even worse, she has over 100 books and novellas with multiple small presses, in science fiction and fantasy, YA, suspense, women's fiction, and sub-genres of romance.

Her official launch into publishing came with winning first place in the Writers of the Future contest in 1990. She was a finalist in the EPIC Awards competition multiple times, winning with *Lorien* in 2006 and *The Meruk Episodes, I-V*, in 2010, and was a finalist in the Realm Awards competition, in conjunction with the Realm Makers convention.

Her training includes the Institute for Children's Literature; proofreading at an advertising agency; and working at a community newspaper. She is a tea snob and freelance edits for a living (MichelleLevigne@gmail.com for info/rates), but only enough to give her time to write. Her newest crime against the literary world is to be co-managing editor at Mt. Zion Ridge Press and launching the publishing co-op, Ye Olde Dragon Books. Be afraid … be very afraid.

www.Mlevigne.com
www.MichelleLevigne.blogspot.com
www.YeOldeDragonBooks.com
www.MtZionRidgePress.com
@MichelleLevigne

Look for Michelle's Goodreads groups:
Guardians of Neighborlee
Voyages of the AFV Defender
Neighborlee Streets

NEWSLETTER:
Want to learn about upcoming books, book launch parties, inside information, and cover reveals?
Go to Michelle's website or blog to sign up.

Also by Michelle L. Levigne

Guardians of the Time Stream: 4-book Steampunk series
The Match Girls: Humorous inspirational romance series starting
    with **A Match (Not) Made in Heaven**
Sarai's Journey: A 2-book biblical fiction series
Tabor Heights: 20-book inspirational small town romance series.
Quarry Hall: 11-book women's fiction/suspense series
For Sale: Wedding Dress. Never Used: inspirational romance
Crooked Creek: Fun Fables About Critters and Kids: Children's
    short stories.
Do Yourself a Favor: Tips and Quips on the Writing Life. A book
    of writing advice.
To Eternity (and beyond): Writing Spec Fic Good for Your Soul. A
    book defending speculative fiction.
Killing His Alter-Ego: contemporary romance/suspense, taking
    place in fandom.
The Commonwealth Universe: SF series, 25 books and growing
The Hunt: 5-book YA fantasy series
Faxinor: Fantasy series, 4 books and growing
Wildvine: Fantasy series, 14 books when all released
Neighborlee: Humorous fantasy series
Zygradon: 5-book Arthurian fantasy series
AFV Defender: SF adventure series
Young Defenders: Middle Grade SF series, spin-off of *AFV Defender*
Magic to Spare: Fantasy series
Book & Mug Mysteries: cozy mystery series starting in 2022
Quest for the Crescent Moon: fantasy series starting in 2022

www.ingramcontent.com/pod-product-compliance
Lightning Source LLC
Chambersburg PA
CBHW010845190726
48286CB00012BA/3005